THE TREE OF
FORGETFULNESS

YELLOW SHOE FICTION

Michael Griffith, *Series Editor*

THE TREE OF FORGETFULNESS

A Novel

PAM DURBAN

Louisiana State University Press
Baton Rouge

Published by Louisiana State University Press
Copyright © 2012 by Louisiana State University Press
All rights reserved
Manufactured in the United States of America
LSU Press Paperback Original
FIRST PRINTING

DESIGNER: Mandy McDonald Scallan
TYPEFACE: Adobe Garamond Pro
PRINTER AND BINDER: McNaughton & Gunn, Inc.

Library of Congress Cataloging-in-Publication Data

Durban, Pam.
 The tree of forgetfulness : a novel / Pam Durban.
   p. cm. — (Yellow shoe fiction)
  ISBN 978-0-8071-4972-0 (pbk. : alk. paper) — ISBN 978-0-8071-4973-7 (pdf) —
ISBN 978-0-8071-4974-4 (epub) — ISBN 978-0-8071-4975-1 (mobi)
 I. Title.
 PS3554.U668T84 2012
 813'.54—dc23

2012017588

The paper in this book meets the guidelines for permanence and durability of the Committee on Production Guidelines for Book Longevity of the Council on Library Resources. ∞

For Peter, always

Where blood has been spilled, the tree of
forgetfulness will not flourish.
—BRAZILIAN PROVERB

Gradually it was disclosed to me that the line separating good
and evil passes not through states, nor between classes,
nor between political parties—but right through every
human heart—and through all human hearts.
—ALEKSANDR SOLZHENITSYN

THE TREE OF
FORGETFULNESS

Howard Aimar

June 1943

YOU DON'T MEAN IT, people will say. Fifty is too young to die. He was such a good father, they will say. Such a good man. Remember Howard at the piano at Christmastime, singing "Joy to the World" with Libba and the children? What a beautiful tenor voice he had, it fit so well with Libba's sweet soprano. Did you ever see him dressed for an evening out? In that white silk scarf and the long, ivory cigarette holder tipped up at a dramatic angle, didn't he look like FDR himself? Remember how, when anyone stopped him on the street to ask, he could talk for ten minutes about how Lewis was getting along over there in the Pacific, fighting the Japanese? You'd think God in His mercy would have spared a father's life until his son came home from war, but as we have been taught so long and so well: God's ways are not our own.

Howard and Libba owned a movie camera, of course, a Bell and Howell, the newest thing, and no matter how he moaned and groaned about that camera, you could tell he was proud that it cost so much; they both were. In a home movie shot in April in the backyard of their big, fine house, he followed his daughter Cecile along a winding path through the azaleas, holding up the long train of that white gown she wore when she was crowned May Queen at St. Angela Academy. Bent like an old man, one hand on his aching back, he mimed the faithful servant hobbling along behind the young monarch; you could tell he was joking by the way he mugged for the camera. Howard was a cutup, a practical joker. And *dance.* That man could do it all—foxtrot, jitterbug, even the Charleston.

In early June the *Aiken Standard* carried an item on the social page: "Mr. and Mrs. Howard Aimar attended the graduation from St. Angela Academy of their daughter, the delightful and charming Miss Cecile Aimar." A week later he was rushed to the hospital in agony, his appendix about to burst. After the hurry-up operation, blood poisoning set in, and three days later, in spite of all the love, the singing, the dancing and clowning, in spite of his son's absence and all the other objections raised against his dying, Howard Aimar was gone.

In the story handed down through the family like an heirloom, negligence, possibly malfeasance, caused the fatal infection, because the sudden death of such a good, generous, fun-loving family man, a man with everything to live for, cannot happen for the simple reason that people are struck down sometimes; there must be a villain, a mistake. They didn't have to look far to find both.

A few months after his death, a nurse who'd been in the operating room that day hinted to Cecile that the doctor might have wiped the scalpel on a not-quite-clean towel. A sponge might have gone into Howard Aimar's body and not come out, though she wouldn't put her hand on the Bible and swear to either fact. They had to get that appendix out, and abdominal surgery was always fraught with the danger of infection, especially in 1943, when penicillin was needed overseas and there was a shortage at home. But over time the dirty scalpel and the lost sponge would become enshrined as the cause of his death and of the mistrust and resentment that still lead Howard Aimar's kin to give the doctor's kin the cold shoulder if they run into them at Sunday brunch at the country club or in the crowd lining Laurens Street to watch the Christmas parade.

But now it is the first of his last three days, and as he lies dying, Howard Aimar goes on making plans, as though planning for the future will save his place there. Doesn't everyone feel too necessary and unfinished to die? Faced with catastrophe, how often do we say, *Wait, stop, there's been a mistake,* and trust that we will be heard and allowed to finish the work we've started or to start the work we're always about to begin?

A cedar grows outside the open window of his hospital room (open because his wife, Dr. Hastings's daughter, insists on fresh air in a sickroom), and early that morning a mockingbird lights in this tree and scribbles a long complicated song in the air. It sings as though singing his plans back to him, the way his secretary, Miss Laura Sudlow, reads the letters he dictates from his desk at Howard Aimar Insurance and Real Estate. Reads them with such spirit that she makes his ideas sound fresh and full of possibility, even in that dim, narrow slot of an office with windows set so high in the walls they frame only sky. His place of business, where no matter how fresh and clear the weather, the air always smells of fuel oil and carbon paper and the ink of typewriter ribbons.

The place would be completely drab if it weren't for the pictures on the walls, like the painting behind Howard's desk that depicts the moment at Waterloo when the British repulsed Napoleon's cavalry and the battle was lost, splashed with the blood of dying men and dying horses, a swarm of red and blue uniforms. That painting had hung above his father's desk in the pharmacy in Augusta where he'd toiled his life away, and he'd felt a special kinship with one dying French soldier. Howard finds the picture appropriate to his situation too, though he sees himself as a British soldier, not a French cavalryman, and he believes that this way of thinking makes him the victor in the battle against despair that his father lost.

Waterloo is framed in gold, more gold surrounds the prints that advertise the insurance companies whose products Howard Aimar sells. From Lincoln Life there is the haggard Lincoln of the war's middle years, and the Fireman's Fund is represented by a scene of a sooty fireman carrying a small blonde angel of a girl out of a burning house. Every morning as he walks past that picture on the way to his desk, his own wife looks back at him out of the child's untroubled blue eyes. *Life is good,* she whispers. *And you, my love, are provider and protector of that goodness.*

Not that Libba's childhood home had ever been threatened by fire.

She grew up in a house with four chimneys, surrounded by a yard full of azaleas and sweet-smelling shrubs, the town's first automobile parked under the porte cochere. She grew up with a brother and a father who petted and spoiled her and a mother who hosted ice cream socials and sang in the First Presbyterian Church choir. A woman who kept the home and served as president of the Choral Club, the Civic Club, and the Little Garden Club, whose yearly flower show she had founded and nurtured into statewide fame.

A woman who contributed her opinions to a column in the *State* newspaper called "As a Woman Thinketh." "For years I have been using a face lotion that my grandmother used before me. She paid fifty cents for it, and it is made by an old chemical concern in New York. I have never been able to find it in a South Carolina drugstore, though she used to buy it anywhere in the state. They will order it for me but charge me a dollar and a quarter for it. I can order it from a retail drugstore in Georgia for seventy-five cents. Shall I pay a druggist fifty cents to write my letter for me? Not while I've got a perfectly good typewriter and don't suffer from rheumatism!"

Her more serious reflections appeared in the *Keystone* magazine published by the Federation of Women's Clubs: "The heart must be developed as well as the head. This necessarily reverts to the home, where the youth must be taught control of the instincts and the obligations to society stressed."

"Spirited," people called Libba's mother, but not so spirited as to be thought hysterical or difficult.

Libba grew up believing she would marry a boy who came from one of the two or three families that Dr. and Mrs. Henderson Hastings judged to be on a par with their own. She hadn't known she needed rescuing until Howard came along. One cool morning in late September the year she'd turned eighteen, she'd been enjoying a walk among the sweetly flowering tea olive bushes in the front yard of her father's house, when she'd heard footsteps on the brick sidewalk outside their fence. A man walked up to the fence and stopped. "What is that heavenly smell?" he said, and she broke off a sprig of tea olive and gave it to him, and in that moment she saw that compared to the man who had stopped at her fence, the boys who walked with her to church and came to her ice cream socials wore the soft, unformed faces of children, and she felt as though she'd stepped into a bright maze where every path led to the same radiant place. Her mother tapped on the front window, but she didn't turn. If the ground had opened at their feet, she would have gladly tumbled with him into the crack.

When I get well, Howard Aimar sings along with the mockingbird, *I will go down to my office and burn those files.* He should have done it long ago, and as he imagines it now, his hands rehearse the tearing and wadding of paper. From somewhere nearby Libba whispers, "What is he doing? Howard, stop." Her hands capture his, but the planning continues. He will collect all the long yellow sheets covered with numbers and sums and dump them into the burning barrel in the alley. He will light a fire and stir it with the scorched rake he keeps beside the barrel, catch each drifting cinder and return it to the flames until he is sure the pages are burnt up and not just charred. He will burn all the pale blue pages of Laura Sudlow's personal stationery as well, the ones with her address embossed at the top, and then the trail will disappear that leads from his office to her small white house behind the camellias, and no one will ever know or be tempted to make up a story about the net they've woven to hold the money that is always tearing, or threatening to tear, in a dozen places or the hours he's spent at her dining room table with his head in his hands, looking for a way to balance the money trickling in with the money gushing out. *When I get well,* the mockingbird sings, *I will pay my just debts and clear my name so that years from now, when I am an old man and dying in my proper time, no one will be ashamed of anything I've done.*

One of Laura Sudlow's letters pleads with him to pay some of the premiums owed to the Fireman's Fund; another reports that Lincoln Life has called for an accounting of delinquent payments. She is the perfect secretary, the ideal confidante. She knows everything and does not judge, except for Libba's spending, and then only in the mildest way. "Maybe Libba could do without a new coat this year?" That is one of the suggestions written in her small, flowing script. "Perhaps

5

you could shorten your trip to the beach this summer, or stay home in good old Aiken for a change?" But the idea of not taking Libba to Waveland, the house on Sullivan's Island that they rent for a month every summer, fills him with clawing panic. If they stay home, Libba will suspect that something is wrong, and Libba must not be suspicious; her faith in life's goodness rests on her faith in him, and he will not betray that faith. Besides, if they don't go to the beach, her mother and father might call out to her from their adjoining graves in Bethany Cemetery. *Castles in the clouds,* they'd say. *We warned you, Libba.* And this time she might listen.

Libba is forty-five the year Howard dies. Every morning before she leaves for the hospital, she dresses in a snug skirt and a freshly pressed blouse and fastens on the pearl necklace he gave her for their first anniversary. "To my pearl of great price," he wrote on the tag in his elegant, beveled script. Three days earlier, coming up from under the anesthesia, he'd grabbed the pearls and held on so tightly she'd thought he would break them. It is one of the stories she will tell the grandchildren, who will know him only through stories: how she had to pry his fingers loose that day, else he would have broken her necklace, and that would have broken her heart.

Today, as every day, she tips a few drops of Chanel No. 5 onto her fingers from one of the bottles he tucks in her Christmas stocking every year and dabs the perfume behind her ears. She pins up her dark hair and spreads bright lipstick on her mouth and stops in the hall outside his room to pinch color into her cheeks before she sashays in and kisses him on the forehead. "Hello, my love," she says, then pulls a chair up close to his bed, pats his arm and laughs her high sweet laugh that ripples in the air like a bright flag on the ramparts of happiness. She touches her pearls and chats about this and that—the back door hinges oiled and the driveway raked, their little flock of Barred Plymouth Rock hens laying eggs all over the yard, the branches of the hundred peach trees in her aunt's orchard so laden they have to be held up with forked sticks. She talks as if this sickness and the deepening gray shadow it throws over his face, the way he lies like a stone king on a tomb, is a passing inconvenience. She will give him, as she has given him ever since the night she climbed out of her bedroom window and ran away with him in a borrowed car across the Savannah River and married him in front of a justice of the peace in Augusta, the gift of her complete confidence.

This morning he manages a word. "Lewis," he says, and she's ready. No new letter has come from their son, so she opens the most recent letter again, unfolding the thin V-mail page and reading around the blacked-out lines. "Dear Folks, All is well and I am healthy and eating well. Yesterday, I ate my first coconut, which is surprisingly tasty once you figure a way to crack that doggone shell. I used the butt of my rifle, which is, I figure, about the most work it's going to get! The army is keeping me pretty busy, but I manage to get in a swim most days in this tropical paradise where they've sent me. Ha-ha."

Hearing Lewis's letter, he remembers more reasons to live. To see Cecile married, to welcome Lewis home, to know his grandchildren, to love his wife through all her days, to make amends for his failures and lacks, to become, finally and completely, the man he meant to be.

As she does every day, Libba sits beside his bed and ticks off on her fingers the food that friends and kin have brought to the house. Ham and chicken and potato salad and succotash and custard, pickled peaches and deviled eggs. When he opens his eyes and sees her hands, he smiles. He loves her hands. Unlike the rest of her—her long slender neck and waist and legs—her hands are small and compact, with short blunt fingers and thick palms, hands made for work, not leisure. "My Lord, Howard, I'm going to turn into a butterball if you don't hurry up and come home to help me eat that food," she says, running her hands over her hips to show him the danger. The sight of her hips makes him smile too. The smell of her perfume brings pictures: curtains stirring at their bedroom window, himself turning the lock on their door.

At noon Cecile looks at her father's hands that lie where they've fallen. "Please stop, Mother. He can't hear you," she says.

"Of course he can, Cecile, don't be foolish." Libba leans over and kisses his forehead. "Look at him smile when I tell him about the food." As long as they both shall live, she will comfort him, and if

Cecile doesn't approve, she can go about her business and leave them in peace.

When his appetite comes back, she tells him, he can eat himself to sleep, and when he wakes up, she'll pop another tidbit in his mouth; she'll fatten him up until he fits into his old cheerful self again. They'll start with pecans, good old Gloria Grandes from their backyard trees, roasted in butter and salt, the way he likes them. Her aunt's peaches will ripen, and every Sunday evening he will churn peach ice cream on the back porch. "Look at him smile about that ice cream, Miss Doubting Thomas," she says to Cecile, raising her voice so that he can hear. This is her last gift to him: trusting as she's always trusted that what seems to be happening is not.

"You won't believe it, Howard," she says. "But Minnie's back. Just for the time being, of course, but never mind." She has come out of the goodness of her heart, Libba says, to answer the door and keep track of the food in a notebook that Libba keeps on the table in the foyer. "Minnie's coming to see you, Howard. She promised," Libba says.

Minnie. Hearing her name, he hears another—Zeke. Fear comes up in him like thick black smoke, and he runs through it, flailing and thrashing. "Help me up," he shouts, but no one hears. He needs to get back to his office and start another fire and burn the papers he saved during the terrible autumn of 1926, when three colored people were killed and a New York reporter came down to accuse them all of murder.

Just before sunset Cecile calls the priest. She and Lewis have been raised Catholic, as their Presbyterian mother had promised their father's church they would be. Cecile knows every Holy Day of Obligation. She recognizes Satan himself, father of lies, in the snake crushed under the cool marble heel of the Virgin Mary's statue. She knows the meaning of all the vestments and bells and candles. She knows when and why they kneel and stand during Mass, why the bishop slaps your face at Confirmation, and how mortal sin destroys the soul. She needs no book to guide her through her examination of conscience before Confession; she has memorized the list of sins against every commandment. She knows when to call the priest.

When he hears the priest's voice, Howard opens his eyes long enough to see the purple stole, but he doesn't know where to start. A voice scribbles away inside him, but it speaks so quietly he can't hear what it's saying. How to confess that you were one man in a swarm of men whose time had handed him easier words than sin or evil to name what he had done or failed to do? How to confess to the silence in which he has wrapped himself for seventeen years? He closes his eyes, moves deeper inside himself, and from that place he sees the room and the bed and himself on the bed. It is strange to feel his body crumble while his mind stays clear and full of light. To feel time move as in a dream, where a day passes in an instant and a whole story flashes by.

At first he thinks the mockingbird has flown into the room. The light flutters as though disrupted by wings, but there is no bird, only a woman who sits beside the bed and looks at him calmly, her long, light hair scattered over the collar of a deep green coat of an unfamiliar cut. "Lewis?" he almost says. With her long, narrow face and imperial nose, she looks so much like his son. His sadness is in her face too, and also his brightness, the brightness of life. She has Lewis's eyes and chin, her grandmother's full mouth, but tugged down at the ends, unlike Libba's. She has her own way of holding her shoulders, but her hands, with their short, competent fingers and thick palms, are Libba's. *Hello, Granddaddy,* she says.

As though by remembering the autumn of 1926, then wishing it away, he's invited or conjured her. The curious grandchild, the one he'd feared, the one who might feel the pull of that history and believe she has the right to collect the fragments and scraps he should have burned and make another story from them about how it was, and who he was and what he did. And it won't do any good to say, *Why dwell on the ugliness of the past? A man has the right to some peace.* When the future comes to demand an accounting from the past, it will not be denied.

2

Curtis N. R. Barrett

October 1926

SOUTH OF RICHMOND, when he was sure the train had crossed the Mason-Dixon Line, he closed the door to the Pullman sleeper, uncapped his flask, and drank and watched the light of the setting sun flash through the dark trees beside the track. In his notebook he found the page of details he'd gathered for the last story he'd written for the *New York World* before leaving for the South. The lines there, written as he watched the police photographers fire their flashbulbs at the couple on the bed, crossed the page at a slant. MR. AND MRS. THOMAS AUSTIN one of them had printed in block letters in the ledger at the Waldorf's front desk. Then they'd gone up to the room, where he had cut her throat and his own. They were young, and they held hands on the blood-soaked satin bedspread, she in her slip, he in his drawers, the straight razor in his free hand and the look in their eyes that he'd seen in the eyes of corpses in France during the Great War: People always seemed startled to find themselves dead.

The boy was pigeon-chested, so thin his ribs showed. The girl's worn leather purse lay open on the nightstand next to a lacquered red Chinese stick, the kind that girls used to anchor twists of long hair. Hers was a rich chestnut brown, worn in the smooth, short bob that was in style now. Where it wasn't heavy with blood, her slip was still creased, probably just unfolded from the Bergdorf's box on the floor. "Fancier than either could afford," he'd written. "Pale cream satin trimmed with lace. 'Candlelight' the salesgirl might have called it."

"Wedding gift?" he'd scribbled. They'd worn rings, so they were married, not necessarily to each other.

He'd been sent to the Waldorf because he was the *World*'s crime reporter, but a note had been fished out of the blood, defiant, printed in the same hand as the names in the desk ledger—they'd chosen this way over the plans that others had made for them—so no crime had been committed, unless you called the willing forfeit of two young lives a crime. Looking down at the bodies on the bed, his pencil moving across the page, he'd found that he did not share the dead couple's surprise at what had happened to them; in fact, he felt nothing but a cold, steady pulse of anger at the fact that they had chosen what so many others had not chosen but what had been done to them anyway.

Home from the war too late for the big parades, he'd gotten off the ship in New York, walked from the docks to Grand Central Station, and bought a ticket to New Bedford, Massachusetts, holding in his mind, as he'd done throughout the war, the image of his father opening the door of the office that waited for him at the mill. Barrett was one of the smaller mills in New Bedford: five hundred spindles turning out a fine cotton lawn. Every one of his father's wartime letters had included a report on the mill's monthly output and an assessment of whether the total yardage met or exceeded or fell short of expectations. He'd closed every letter with the same words: "Son," he wrote. "You must not worry about where you will go or what you will do to make a living when you come home. Do not allow yourself to be distracted or burdened over there by uneasy thoughts about your future here." His signature had occupied the bottom third of the page.

Curtis N. R. Barrett returned to the States on a cool day, but as he walked along the platform looking for an uncrowded car, he started to sweat. Every window teemed with faces and hands pressed to the glass, and images of the mill came to him—flying spindles, steel fingers rising and falling, picking and twisting. He was still in uniform, the red cross of the medical corps on both sleeves, and whenever he looked up at the train, people smiled down at him or nodded solemnly, as though they knew him. In one car a woman held a little boy up to the window and pointed. The boy waved and smiled and saluted, and when he only waved back, the child pouted and hid his face in his mother's shoulder. No doubt, once the train was moving, and the only way off was to jump, the woman and the boy would walk through the cars until they found him, and then they would stand there and wait for him to return the salute the boy was owed.

He could not trust himself to be reasonable if that happened, so he cashed in his ticket, rented a room. A few days later, reading the *New York World* in a coffee shop in Times Square, he'd come across Joseph Pulitzer's statement on the mission of his newspaper: "An institution that should always fight for progress and reform, never tolerate injustice or corruption, always fight demagogues of all parties, never belong to any party, always oppose privileged classes and public plunderers, never lack sympathy with the poor, always remain devoted to the public welfare, never be satisfied with merely printing news, always be drastically independent, never be afraid to attack wrong, whether by predatory plutocracy or predatory poverty." The hard, clear certainty of it had moved him, and he'd realized it wasn't just the flying spindles he couldn't go back to; it was the piety of the Sunday dinner table as well, the prime rib and Potatoes Anna, his father's interminable prayer for the well-being of his business. A few days later he wired home: "Detained in NY. Don't wait up."

"God bless and keep you, son," his father had wired back. "Come home when you can." He hadn't expected more.

Carrying the hard black case that held his typewriter, he stepped down from the train in Aiken, South Carolina, walked through the station and out the double doors at the front. He set the case down under the portico. He took a cigarette out of a silver case and tapped it on the case and lit up, blew the smoke straight up into the air. *Take a good look.* People would be watching, Leland had said. Count on it. A porter followed, pushing a handcart on which were piled two brown leather suitcases with CNRB stamped in gold just above the handle. He gave the man a dollar bill, went back to smoking. The sun slanted through pines and palmettos at a low, early-morning angle. In a small oak beside the station, blue jays squabbled; a smell of woodsmoke hung in the air.

Curtis N. R. Barrett, what kind of name was that? people eating lunch at the counter at the Savoy would say to one another, throwing their napkins down in disgust. It suits him right well, they'd say; it matches the vanity of the thick, wavy hair combed back just so, the dark vest and trousers and white shirt, the silver cuff links and collar pin, the dark glasses and that signet ring on the pinkie finger of the hand that brought the cigarette up to his mouth and down again. Another big shot New York reporter come to tar a community of decent people for the actions of the lawless few. He stood in front of the station, smoking, and watched the fountain splash. *Take a good damn look.* A few people did, slowing their cars. A man in overalls driving a wagon pulled by two dusty mules stared at him as he passed then turned his head to keep looking. The breeze picked up and rustled the fronds of the palmettos in front of the station. He smelled breakfast in the air.

Two days earlier his editor, Bayard Swope, had summoned him to his office. "King of the *World,*" reporters called Swope. It was a joke, but also true. His window offered a king's vista—the East River and the Brooklyn Bridge, with its symphony of cables. Swope was a famous gambler, lucky at horses and cards, and an equally famous reporter. Three years earlier, in a marathon poker game in a private railway car in Palm Beach, he'd relieved two rich men of close to half a million dollars. On one office wall he'd hung framed clippings from the coverage of that triumph, and right alongside them his 1917 Pulitzer Prize citation, for a series of articles called "Inside the German Empire."

But Swope was happy to share the wealth. He sat behind the same rough desk where he'd always written, was generous with his Cuban cigars. He knew a story that needed telling when he saw one, like the one Leland Dawson had brought back from South Carolina. The story had begun in April 1925, when Sheriff Earl Glover was shot and killed during a liquor raid on a family of tenant farmers named Long.

Bessie Long, her brother Dempsey, and their cousin Albert had been arrested, tried, and found guilty of killing the sheriff. The boys were sentenced to the electric chair, the girl to life in prison, and that would have been the end of it if N. R. Latham, one of the few black lawyers in South Carolina, hadn't filed appeal after appeal with the state supreme court until finally, in October 1926, the Longs were sent back to Aiken for a new trial. N. R. Latham had showed up there too, along with a white lawyer from Spartanburg, to argue their case. On the third day of that second trial the judge directed a not-guilty verdict against Dempsey, but before nightfall he'd been picked up again and charged with assault and battery. Later on that moonless night the electric line to the jail was cut; a mob invaded, seized the Longs, drove them out of town, and shot them to death in front of a crowd of so many witnesses it was hard to believe the whole town hadn't been there.

Of the forty lynchings Leland Dawson had investigated, this was the worst he'd seen. *Depraved* he called what had happened that night in Aiken, and since Leland was careful with language, they'd trusted that the word accurately reflected the fact. Someone had slipped Leland a copy of the report of the coroner's physician, and Leland had given it to Barrett. He'd read it again in the Pullman car heading south, preparing himself.

Albert Long. Shot with shotgun under chin to the left. No. 8 shot.

Dempsey (Son) Long. .38 cal. entered front Breast, came out left of spine in back, four inches left of shoulder blade.

Bessie Long Cheetam. Powder burns on back (left shoulder blade). Pistol wound on right temple .38 cal. lead bullet, entrance of bullet on left side of head two inches above ear going through brain. Each wound sufficient to cause death.

They'd been killed sometime after midnight on the eighth of October, and in the morning their bodies had been loaded onto a county truck and buried in a common grave behind a church near Monetta. Later that day the coroner's jury had questioned Sheriff Aubrey Timmerman about the mob that had taken his prisoners from his jail.

Did you have your flashlight in your hand?
Yes, sir, I did, but I dropped it.
Did you recognize anybody?
All I saw had something on their faces.
Did they have on citizens' clothes?
I didn't pay any attention to the clothes.
They didn't have a Ku Klux robe on?
No, sir.

On October 10 the coroner's jury ruled that the Longs had died at the hands of persons unknown.

The other thing that still amazed them in New York was how Leland Dawson, a black man, secretary of the NAACP, had gotten out of South Carolina alive. He'd posed as a reporter for the *World*, and he was so light-skinned that he'd fooled them. Fooled the white people, anyway; Leland never said if the black people knew he was one of them. Believing they were talking to another white man, two types of people confided in Leland. People with outraged consciences, and thank God for them, he said. There were more of them than he'd let himself hope there would be. And the people who always cluster around a big story like flies around a spill because they want to put themselves in the middle of it, to show how important they are.

Whatever their reasons, people talked to Leland; they named the men who'd dragged the Longs out and driven them up the Columbia Highway and shot them dead, and Leland had sent those names to Governor Arthur McCormick. Then he'd hightailed it back to New York and waited for the South Carolina papers—the *State* and the *Columbia Record* and the *Aiken Standard*—to report that the governor had opened an investigation.

"The eyes of the civilized world are upon Aiken, and her people, innocent as well as guilty, are upon trial," Judge Marvin Mann said in his charge to the grand jurors called into special session on October 18 to investigate the murders.

That had seemed promising, but then the state fair opened in Columbia, and the front page of the *State* filled up with stories about lancing tournaments, and horse races, and the "Hail, South Carolina" pageant that promised to dramatize South Carolina history in its entirety, accompanied by an orchestra and a chorus of eight hundred and fifty voices.

A letter arrived for Leland Dawson, and for a few days they distracted themselves in the newsroom with dramatic readings by anyone who could do a passable southern accent.

Dear Sir:

Mr. Austin Eubanks said in his caustic article in the Aiken Standard that "Leland Dawson, a Negro, came down here and passed himself off as a white man." Is that true? At the time, I had on amber colored glasses and did not study your color, but I took you for a white man and according wto South Carolina law, you may well be.

As you may know, we have a miscegenation law on the books in this State. The Courts had to construe that law and they held that a child born to a black person and a white person is a mulatto. The offspring of a quadroon and a white person is an octoroon, but the child of an octoroon and a white person is WHITE. That's the law of South Carolina, though sometimes the lines get so crossed and re-crossed it is hard to determine exactly what a person is.

But had you been as black as the hinges of hell, I would have treated you exactly as I did. We attend to business for black people, meet with them in our offices, and sometimes when necessary take them into our houses, ride with them in automobiles, and so forth, and never think anything about it.

As a youngster, I heard an amusing story about an argument between two men, one of whom was very dark. An old South Carolina law held that you could not slander someone by calling him a Negro, because everybody could see that he was NOT; but it was slanderous to call him a mulatto. The man quarreling with the dark complexioned man said:

"You are a damned 'latter—NO nigger, nigger, nigger!!!!"
Well, this long letter simply because I want to hear the truth
about what you did or said to persuade people you were white.
And then do the figuring and see what you really are in South
Carolina.

I am, yours very truly for justice to all,
Earl P. Henderson

At the end of every reading they'd laugh about the pompous old cracker, and Leland would remind them that this was the same man who'd tried to warn the judge that lynching was in the air on the day the charges against Dempsey Long were dismissed and he walked out of that courtroom, a free man. But that didn't stop them from laughing the next time the letter was read. "Go on and laugh," Leland always said. He was tempted to join in himself, but he wanted them to understand that it was easier to parse these things from New York than it had been when he was down there in the thick of it, where friend and enemy switched places daily.

On October 28 the grand jury reported to the judge that it was unable to secure sufficient evidence on which to bring indictments and asked to be excused. The *State* reported the story on the third page. That was the day that Swope called Barrett into his office. When he saw the *State* newspaper on Swope's desk, Barrett said, "I'm on my way, boss."

"Can you believe these people?" Swope said, tapping the newspaper.

"No," he said, but that wasn't exactly true. It was what Swope wanted to hear, but he could believe anything now. He believed, for instance, that there was no limit to the harm people could inflict on one another. On any given day during the war, he thought he'd seen the worst. The day when the two men on either side of him had simply dissolved was the nadir, and then the day at Chemin de Fer, when the Germans came over the hill with flamethrowers. Nightfall had brought a kind of relief; surely nothing more awful could come than what had happened that day. But gradually, grindingly, he came to see that what he'd believed were discrete and finite events were parts of an endless series, and every day began from a benchmark slightly more horrific than the one he'd passed the day before.

After meeting with Swope, he'd gone home and packed fast, as though the story were melting ice. Ink pens and yellow paper, his typewriter and clothes. He'd latched the suitcases and stood them by the door. He'd smoothed the white chenille spread then sat on the bed and looked around. An armchair upholstered in flowered chintz, a mahogany dresser and bedstead, a lamp, a table, a sink and mirror on the wall. Already the room felt like he had never lived there, which was how he liked to leave things. When he walked out the door, carrying his suitcases and his typewriter, there would be no trace of him left.

A wagon pulled by a shaggy chestnut horse with white front feet eased under the portico in front of the station, and a tall young black man jumped down and walked toward Barrett with a long stride, his fists clenched at his sides. He was dressed in a black suit coat, a faded blue shirt buttoned up under his chin, dusty gray pants mended with thick white thread, and a pair of brogans laced with brown twine. A gray fedora was cocked over one eye.

"Carry you somewhere, captain?" he said, pulling off the hat. He had a deep voice, and he pronounced every word completely, as though competing in elocution. His face was rough, like a rock outcrop, and he had a way of looking just to the side of Barrett's eyes with a grim little smile that seemed meant to be humble but felt challenging. He looked, Barrett thought, like a man who had just lost one fight and didn't plan to lose the next one. Given what Leland had said about this place, he bet that look had gotten him into plenty of trouble.

The black man pointed behind him, to the wagon. Barrett tugged down his vest, straightened his tie, dusted off his shirt and trousers. "You bet," he said. "Take me to the Hotel Aiken." The hotel stood directly across Park Avenue from the Southern Railway depot, but he didn't want to be seen carrying his own suitcases across the sandy street. The young man gave him a quick, narrow look from the corner of one eye then shrugged; he was used to carrying white men across the street, out into the county, ten times around the block; as long as they paid him, it wasn't any of his business where they wanted to go. He had the biggest hands Barrett had ever seen.

He settled the hat back on his head, picked up both suitcases and tucked one under his arm, then picked up the typewriter case and clumped off toward the wagon. Barrett followed him out from under the portico and into the light. A haze of woodsmoke hung in the air, the rich, fermenting smell of rotting leaves. White sand below and a bright blue sky overhead, the moon still hanging in the sky like an empty bowl. The gleam of pine needles in the sunlight and the squawk of blue jays hauled him back to the moment when he'd stepped off another train and into the same light and air, down in Georgia, where they'd sent him to learn to shoot and climb, to dig and run and hit the dirt, and burrow into it. Where he'd volunteered for the medical corps, learned to splint bones and pack wounds and swab gas from men's eyes and skin. "Curtis N. R. Barrett," he said, putting out his hand. The man looked around then shook Barrett's hand once and dropped it. "What's your name?" Barrett asked, as they stood beside the wagon.

The question seemed to startle him. He kept his eyes on Barrett's face as he spat to one side. "Zeke," he said.

"I thought you looked familiar. Didn't I see your picture in the *Aiken Standard* a few weeks back?"

Zeke looked at him obliquely again, calculating. "Might could have. Get on up there if you please, sir."

"I thought so," he said as he climbed up. *A familiar sight,* the caption beneath the picture of a smiling Zeke and his wagon had read. He was ashamed of himself for feeling relieved that the question had rattled Zeke. Ten minutes in the South, and he wanted to gain the upper hand.

Zeke loaded his suitcases and the typewriter case into the bed of the wagon then climbed up onto the seat beside him. "Come to think of it," Barrett said, "why don't you take me for a turn around the metropolis before we go to the hotel."

"Yes, sir," Zeke said, grinning. "I am happy to do that." He clucked at the horse and flapped the reins, and they started off down a wide dirt street that was separated from a parallel street by a park planted in plume grass and small oaks held up by guy-wires.

"Pretty town," Barrett said.

Zeke touched the brim of his hat. "Yes, sir," he said. "It is."

Barrett knew this kind of Negro, more and more of them coming to New York all the time. You could guess how long they'd been there by how careful they were not to offend. A month or less, and they still doffed their hats, stepped off the sidewalk to let a white man pass, looked at the ground when they talked. "You're in the North now, son," he'd said to the new man from Alabama who swept up at the paper.

"Yes, sir," he'd answered, keeping his eyes on the floor. "Much obliged."

Zeke's wagon rolled along the street, wheels hissing through the sand. A light hack passed them, pulled by a gleaming bay horse outfitted in an oiled harness with polished brass buckles and jingling hardware. A sharp-faced woman sat up very straight on the seat, holding a thin whip with a silver handle and looking straight ahead. She wore a hunting horn on a red cord around her neck, an African helmet on her head. As she passed, Zeke tipped his hat. "Morning, Mrs. Hitchcock," he said.

"Zeke," she said, without turning her head, as though driving the horse demanded all her attention. His horse nickered, and the woman smiled. "You too, Princess," she said.

Once she was ahead of them, Zeke said, "I haul ice cream to that lady's parties. She doesn't believe in iceboxes. Rich lady from up North. A whole slew of them come here every year. When she was a puny little girl, her auntie brought her here to take the cure, and by the time she got well, she liked it so much she decided to keep on coming. Brought all her friends down here with her too."

"What do people need curing of, Zeke?" he asked.

Zeke pressed one big hand to his chest. "Consumption, Mr. Barrett. TB. The hotels and boardinghouses fill up with them every year. They get well here too," he said. "They surely do that." Every spring he beat the rugs from the hotels and boardinghouses that catered to the tubercular pilgrims. He bundled up the bed linens and took them to his mother and the other women who boiled and washed them. People hired him for any kind of errand. *Go meet the Columbia train and pick up a package and bring it to my house. Go to the icehouse for me, chop-chop.* He saved thick chunks of oak so his mother could keep a slow fire going under the kettles behind her house in Howard Aimar's backyard; he brought the laundry to her and took it back when it was done. On horse trading Tuesdays he went to a flat, sandy lot behind Laurens Street called the Boneyard and laid out his blacksmith's tools on an old blanket. He hired out his wagon for children's birthday hayrides, wore a silk top hat and morning coat for those occasions.

"When the rich folks come to town, you can go down there to Hahn's Grocery and buy you any kind of special cheese you want," he said.

"You're a good tour guide," Barrett said.

"Thank you, sir."

Across the long narrow park between the streets he saw the Catholic church then the courthouse and the wall of the jail behind it. Barrett had read about the sickly and the healthy rich, their horses and their cheese and English biscuits. They called Aiken "the village," and the locals treated them like visiting royalty or gods on a mountaintop, and they were the mortals below, telling stories about the deities. He disliked lords and ladies as much as any New Englander. "Listen here," he said, leaning over close to Zeke's ear. "You know anyplace I can buy some whiskey?" The supply he'd brought from New York would be gone in a week, but there would be good whiskey here, the nobility would have seen to that too; the local product wouldn't be good enough for them. Leland said there was top-notch blockade whiskey being smuggled up the Savannah River and into town.

Zeke shifted suddenly on the wagon seat and flapped the reins over the horse's back. "No, sir," he said. "I wouldn't know about that, but I'll tell you who does. You remember that jail we passed back there?" he jerked his thumb over his shoulder. "It's full up all the time with whiskey people, men and women both. Sheriff Timmerman takes a particular interest in the whiskey business. He'll run you down, sure enough, you start messing with that whiskey. But if you need your clothes kept up, my mother does that for folks all over town. I pick up on Saturday, deliver back to you on Wednesday."

"I will need that," he said. "Much obliged. But I'd like to find some decent whiskey too."

"I don't know about that, sir, I surely don't," Zeke said. "You need anything else, ask for Zeke. That's Ezekial Settles," he said slowly, as though Barrett might be writing it down. He chirped to the horse and flicked the reins on her broad, dusty back. "Get up there, lazybones," he said. They had reached Laurens, the town's main street, a wide dirt track lined with wooden and brick buildings and a line of gingko trees down both sides. Their golden leaves fluttered against the bright blue sky.

"My God," Barrett said.

"The wife of my employer planted them trees," Zeke said. "I dug every one of those holes. You wait till you see those leaves come showering down like gold falling out the sky."

A few wagons and a couple of square black Fords were angled into parking places along the curb on either side of the thoroughfare. A line of tracks ran down the middle of the sandy street. "You have a trolley here," Barrett said.

"Sure do," Zeke answered, relieved, Barrett saw, to be a tour guide again. "Runs all the way down through the valley and across the river over to Augusta and back. You can set your watch by it."

"Well, I'll be damned," Barrett said. "Isn't that something?"

"Yes, sir, it is."

They rolled down Laurens Street, past a shop displaying hats on stands in the window. Out front a girl in a long gray skirt and a white blouse cranked down a gold-and-white striped awning. She shaded her eyes and watched them pass, and when Barrett nodded, she looked away. Outside of the hardware store, talking and laughing, two black men dragged heaters onto the street. At least there's money here, Barrett thought. And some of the black people were prosperous: doctors, teachers, tailors, builders, butchers. Leland had been excited to talk about that. They could go to a good school, the Schofield Normal and Industrial School, that had been operating since just after the Civil War. Thank God it wasn't some sun-whipped cotton town with a few grand houses behind magnolia trees, a cotton gin, and a water tank up on rickety stilts. He'd seen enough of those towns from the train. He'd seen enough cotton fields too, the spindly brown plants picked clean, the shacks in the middle of the stubble, half-naked children and skinny dogs in the bare yards. The worst sight had been the abandoned tracts with their deep, eroded gullies, a wasted landscape where ignorance and carelessness had done the same work the shells and bombs had done in France. The deeper into the South the train had traveled, the lower he'd felt, as though he were entering a low-pressure system of the spirit.

Here he could almost smell the complacency in the air, and he felt knives sharpening inside him. The idea of the three Longs dumped into a common grave while people let down gold-and-white awnings and worshipped the rich reminded him of why he'd come. Looking at the couple on the bed at the Waldorf, he'd felt nothing; now he was reckless with the thought that he might be the one to bring justice to these other dead. "Look here," he said. "I guess it was whiskey that started that business with the Longs."

Zeke shifted on the seat, and something watchful happened to his face. "I wouldn't know about that business either, Mr. Barrett," he said. "I surely would not know about that." He clucked and whistled to the horse. "Get up there, you," he said. Already Barrett had ignored Leland's sternest warning. Talking to the black people about the Longs could bring the worst kind of trouble down onto them, he said. Leave them out of this. Do not for one minute forget where you are.

On the stoop in front of a narrow glass door, a man stood watching them, his hands shoved deep in his trouser pockets. Zeke lifted his hand. "How you this morning, Mr. Howard?" he shouted.

The man shrugged. "Comme ci, comme ça," he said, watching Barrett.

"That's Mr. Howard Aimar," he said. "And that's his car. It's one of the new colors." A deep green Ford was parked at the curb. "I work for him too, me and my mother both. I carry his son to school every morning of this world. I'm head on over there soon as I drop you off."

Barrett checked his watch. Seven o'clock. "He go to work this early every morning?" he asked. He turned on the wagon seat to look, but the stoop was empty. The sun had barely cleared the trees; it struck the glass storefronts and gilded the gold letters on the office door. HOWARD AIMAR, INSURANCE AND REAL ESTATE.

"He's a hardworking man, for sure."

And then they pulled up in front of the hotel, and Zeke jumped down, lifted the suitcases out, closed his hand around the money Barrett held out to him. He touched the brim of his hat again. "Much obliged," he said. "Ezekial Settles, at your service."

3

Howard Aimar

June 1943

L IBBA HAS BROUGHT the photograph and set it on the metal
table beside his bed so it's the first thing he sees when he opens
his eyes. One look is all it takes, and he carries the image into
the dark behind his eyes again, where he can study the scuppernong
arbor in her father's yard and the three of them standing under it on
the morning of Lewis's christening. He sees the sunlight dapple Libba's
white high-necked dress, his stiff white dress shirt, the long white gown
in which Hastings babies were always baptized.

This morning, though, when he closes his eyes Libba walks away
from him, carrying Lewis away. "Where are you going with the baby?"
he shouts after her, and her voice drifts down and buzzes in his head
like a wasp trapped in a window.

"Howard," she says, "Howard, lie still. Someone help me." Hands
that are not Libba's press him into the bed and hold him. But Lewis's
daughter is not bothered by his fear; she sits quietly beside his bed,
holding his hand, waiting. Waiting for him to tell what she's come to
hear. And he must do it. She will not wait forever, and somehow he
understands that if she leaves, he will go too. His life, he tells himself,
depends on keeping her there.

Who knows what the dying know, what they feel or what they
think? Dying, we believe, is all ebbing and confusion, but what if the
mind stays clear enough to watch the body go? What if there is a final
alchemy, consciousness refining itself in the fire and turmoil of the
body's failure?

"No matter where we go or what we add or subtract later," he says to her, "we must start with the fact that one of the Longs shot Earl Glover dead when he went to their house that April day in 1925. The Aiken paper got it spot-on right. 'Over a thousand citizens viewed the spot of Sheriff Glover's murder. They saw him lying dead with 93 shots in his back. They saw the door of the Long house splintered with bullets when Dempsey Long engaged Deputy Timmerman and Deputy Bell in battle, shooting first at one and then at the other. They saw the bleeding hand of Timmerman, with an ounce chunk of his flesh torn away by Bessie Long in her effort to kill him with the dead sheriff's pistol, which she had taken from his cold hand . . . You could not tell these people that the Longs were not guilty.'"

"Guilty," he says. "They were guilty as sin, and all of us who endured their second trial over a year later knew what it was like to have that truth defiled. For three days the men in the courtroom, myself and Dr. Hastings among them, watched the lawyer Wise, who'd come all the way down from Spartanburg to argue those people's case, make a big show of rolling up his shirtsleeves, like he was any other honest man going to work. For three days we watched that man strut back and forth in front of Sheriff Glover's widow and orphaned children, braying that the original case against the people who'd killed their husband and father was full of holes so big your could drive a Packard through them. 'Old grandfathers,' he called the court-appointed Aiken lawyers who'd defended the Longs at the first trial.

"And then, as if that man's insults and strutting weren't bad enough, things got much worse when N. R. Latham started talking, and the longer he talked, the thicker the air got, and hotter and harder to breathe, until it felt like a thunderstorm was building inside that courtroom while outside the windows a cool, blue fall day went on about its business.

"Not one scintilla of evidence of a conspiracy to kill the sheriff had ever been introduced, this N. R. Latham said, and since conspiracy had not been proved, all three Longs could not be guilty, as this court had found them in the mockery of a first trial. Throughout Latham's argument Dr. Hastings thumped his cane on the dark wooden floor, like men all over the courtroom were doing, but Latham pitched his voice above the sound and went right on talking.

"It was the word *scintilla* that crawled into my ear and started buzzing. When the judge recessed the court soon after Latham uttered it, I walked over to my office and pulled down the *Webster's* dictionary from the shelf behind my desk and looked up the word. 'A spark, a particle, a trace,' it read. That was all the respect this N. R. Latham had for the truth of the Longs' guilt. I've often thought I'd like to find N. R. Latham now, ask him how he liked the fire that spark started. 'Your own people were the ones who got burnt,' I'd say. 'What do you think about that?'

"After the judge dismissed the guilty verdict against Dempsey Long and adjourned the court, I wanted more than anything to drive Dr. Hastings to his house and then go home myself, to my paper, my supper, my son, my wife, and my bed. But Dempsey Long would not stop grinning or talking or shaking N. R. Latham's hand, and every time I heard Latham's voice, I remembered that word *scintilla* and what it meant, and I got riled up all over again at that colored lawyer in his good suit, and soon, without knowing exactly how it happened, I found myself and Dr. Hastings in the crowd of men who flooded out of the courthouse and ended up in a lawyer's office across the street."

"Because I had to," he says. "Because that's the way the tide was running. If you've ever been caught in a riptide, then you know that you can't swim against it. You'll wear yourself out and drown trying. I expect your father taught you—because I taught both my children—if you're caught in a current, you go with it until you can ease yourself around crossways to the current, then you can swim clear of it.

"So I let that current carry me into the lawyer's office. What does it matter now whose office it was? When no more men could fit inside, someone pulled down the thick yellow shades over the front windows; someone closed and locked the door. And I waited for a chance to work myself crossways to the current that had carried us there. These men were not strangers to me, no. Most of them were men I saw, men who saw me, every day on Laurens Street. Men I knelt beside in church and sat beside at the Rotary Club meetings, who trusted me to sell their homes and insure their lives against catastrophe. But I couldn't name names now, no. My memory's not that clear.

"Dr. Hastings was shaking, his face was brick red, and my first concern was to find him a chair and bring him a drink of water. 'By God,' the old man kept saying. 'By God.' By the time I got him settled, the men in the room were saying that Dempsey had flown the coop, but the sheriff was out looking for him now, to serve him with a warrant for assault and battery that he'd dug up. Before nightfall Dempsey would be back in jail with the rest of his murdering kin, one man said, all three of them locked up safe and sound, and what are we going to do about that? And before I knew what was happening, the men were talking guns.

"'Now hold on just a minute,' I said when the man next to me finished talking. 'Let's think this thing through. Let's take them out of jail and up to Monetta. We'll round up the whole sorry family, hustle them out to the county line, and kick them across and tell them that their shack, their plows, their mules, every last one of their possessions, is forfeit, and they're never to set foot in Aiken County again.'

"A couple of men nodded as I spoke, and when I was done, one or two raised their hands, as though they were voting with me. But the rest folded their arms and studied the carpet like they'd never seen a threadbare Oriental rug before. 'Count me out,' I said. That was when Dr. Hastings offered me the .45 that his own father had made good use of at Gettysburg. The one sent home to the family after the Wilderness by another soldier, whose letter is still kept in the gun case, tucked under the velvet lining. The gun that Dr. Hastings himself carried, eleven years after the war, when he rode with the Red Shirts at Hamburg to break up the Reconstruction government and put the white man back on top.

"He offered, but I refused. There was no call or need for guns, I said. And the whole time I talked, I felt Dr. Hastings studying me the way he'd been studying me since I took Libba across the Savannah River to Georgia and brought her back my wife. *Is he for us or against us?* he was thinking. *Is he one of us or not?*

"That was the question every man in this town had to answer in those days, the one he must answer now and go on answering until the last breath leaves his body and he rests in peace. Because men stand together here, they speak with one voice and act with one will, and the hand of one is the hand of all. When a choice is presented to you that clearly—are you for us or against us? are you one of us or not?—how would you answer? And don't be so quick to say you know, because you don't.

"Which is not to say that some of our own didn't turn against us. Even some of the South Carolina papers printed letters and editorials about us from people who felt high and mighty enough to place blame. 'There is a great company of men down in Aiken who know they are murderers,' one man wrote. 'And knowing that, they have destroyed their own self-respect. They will live and die knowing full well that they are not worthy to associate with their wives and children and are entitled to no respect from decent people. They have fixed their own penalty.'

"Of course I resented that. We all did. Because they had no right, that's why. And I say to you now what I said to your grandmother then, and a hundred times since: Thank God I am not one of those men. Not then, not now, not ever. And to prove it, I will walk you through it. I will take you where I went that night and after so that you will know the truth and it will make you free.

"It was after midnight when I went downstairs and sat at the kitchen table and slipped on my brand-new dress shoes.

"Do you think I don't know I had no business wearing them? Well, because I didn't want to rummage and wake Libba, and they were the first pair that came to hand when I reached into the bedroom closet.

"When I had my shoes on and laced up tight, I made my way across the kitchen, taking care to miss the squeaky spots. With one hand I squelched the small bell that hung at the top of the kitchen door, opened the door with the other, stepped out onto the screened porch there, and closed the door behind me. God, it was dark that night, moon no bigger than a paring, but I knew where I was and what was all around me. A set of unpainted wooden shelves stood against the far wall, lined with Libba's canning jars and flowerpots, all neatly stacked, the way Libba likes things kept. Next to the shelves was a wooden crate full of kindling and small sticks, ranked by length and thickness. The air on that porch smelled richly of pine, and I stood for a while, breathing it in, until I remembered why I was going out that night. I was going for your grandmother and for your father. I was going for Dr. Hastings too, who was no longer young enough to ride around the county late at night, keeping the peace and righting wrongs like the one that had been done us that very afternoon when the colored lawyer stood in that courtroom, bold as brass, and told us there was not one scintilla of evidence against those three murderers and convinced the judge to set one of them free.

"I went to the jail that night—I'm not ashamed to say it—but that's as far as I went. I had to park at my office and walk three blocks to the courthouse, that's how many cars were parked along the streets that night. But when I saw those people brought down, it turned my stomach, and so I did not go where everyone else was going; I went back to my office, and I stayed there."

"What did I do? What does it matter what I did while I was there?" he says. "Call it what you like. Say: 'For the rest of the night he worked his way through the pile of paperwork in the wire basket on his desk. He wrote checks and signed letters and initialed contracts. From time to time he went out and stood on the stoop and watched Orion climb one side of the sky while the new moon fell down the other.'

"I worked all night, and at first light I went home. Libba was waiting for me in the front room. She was wearing her old green flannel bathrobe, and her hair was down around her shoulders, and when she saw me, she jumped up and ran to me. She wrapped her arms around me and held me tight. 'Oh, thank God,' she said, when I told her what I've told you. 'Thank God.' She must have said it half a dozen times.

"Because I didn't go—what else would she have to thank God about?

"'The many innocent cannot be held responsible for the irresponsible actions of the guilty few.' Austin Eubanks, editor of the Aiken paper, wrote in an editorial the week after that night. Libba cut the story out of the paper and put it next to my plate at breakfast time.

That's the kind of wife she has always been to me."

"That's all I have to say, for now," he says, and then he stops, while *for now, for now* tolls in his mind, frightening him. *Now* promises a *later*, when more words will come, and yet it feels as if the words he's just spoken are the last in line; what's left is a fog of silence spreading and deepening inside him the way dusk moves across a field.

4

Curtis N. R. Barrett

November 1926

"**A**N AMBULANCE DRIVER?" some people asked when they learned he'd served in the medical corps, and every time he had to calm himself before he could explain that he had not been a college boy, doing his bit at the rear. He'd been a boy, that much was true—nineteen when he shipped out for France—but he was a medic. He'd carried a bag of tourniquets, needles, and powders as he'd charged, unarmed, toward the German lines, along with his armed comrades, who begged and screamed for him to piece them back together after the machine guns ripped them apart. He did not even attempt to tell the bystanders who gawked at his service that every time he climbed out of the trenches with the other men and lined up for the charge, he watched the muzzles of the German 8's swing around to point at the red cross on his uniform. This morning in his room at the Hotel Aiken, he'd felt amazed and ashamed to see his reflection in the mirror above the small sink where he was shaving.

Now, as he did every morning, he stood at the window and looked across Park Avenue to the Southern Railway depot, where a varying group of men from Leland Dawson's list of perpetrators waited to collect newspapers out of the bundles unloaded from the Columbia train. The "Famous Seventeen," Leland had called the men who planned and carried out the Long killings, and Howard Aimar had not been one of them, but every morning there he was, standing a little way down the platform from the rest, taking no part in the backslapping, the quick, urgent conversations they held with one another.

Thanks to Zeke, those men's names were attached to faces now. For five days after Barrett arrived in town, whenever Zeke drove him somewhere in his wagon, he wore a top hat and frock coat, as though driving Barrett were an honor and a celebration. "Morning, Mr. Manning. Hope you're keeping well, boss," he'd called out loudly, tipping his brim to the man in the tweed hat walking the white collie. The man nodded, fuming, and walked faster, and Barrett understood that he'd just met James Lee Manning, reporter for the *Augusta Chronicle,* author of the letter in the *Aiken Standard* that blamed the lawyer Wise for riling up Aiken's citizens by strutting and bragging in front of Sheriff Glover's widow and orphaned children. "Close around," Leland had written next to Manning's name.

"Evening, Mr. Owen, sir," Zeke said to the rotund man with the heavy-lidded eyes standing on the courthouse steps.

"On your way to the ball, are you, Zeke?" the man said. Deputy Arthur Owen, Barrett thought.

Surely, Barrett thought, Zeke wasn't deliberately pointing out the men on Leland's list; he couldn't know who was on it, and he yelled out to almost everyone they passed, black or white. After a week on Zeke's wagon, Barrett could recognize the black meat merchant John Bush and the builder Wesley Ford, and he knew their stories too; he knew that Ezra Jones tailored riding habits for the rich and that the black druggist, Dr. M. M. Hampton, had sold quinine to the government during the war. Still, he remembered Leland's warning, and he was sure that Leland would say that just by pointing out these men, Zeke had put himself in danger. So one day he said, "No need to name names, Zeke. I can't keep track of them all."

"Can't?" Zeke shouted, amazed. "Well, what's that notebook for?" After that he wore his overalls and a faded blue shirt, shouted mostly at his horse.

Every day for two weeks Barrett made his rounds, in Zeke's wagon or alone, on foot. He went to Finley's Lumberyard, where the air was full of flying sawdust. He stood next to a tall stack of yellow pine boards beaded with resin and shouted questions to Jesse Finley over the high, ringing whine of the saws. "I understand you were tending the drying kiln that night," he said, pointing to the tin shed leaking smoke from every crack and seam. "And you didn't see or hear anything unusual?" Finley cupped his hand to one ear, shook his head.

He went out to Gregorie's cotton gin and shouted his questions over the clanking roar of the machinery, imagined his words smothered in the lint that clung to every surface there. Then back to Hahn's for a conversation about English biscuits and on to Holley Hardware, where nobody would wait on him, no matter how long he stood at the front counter, holding a paper bag of tenpenny nails or a peppermint stick taken from the big clear jar beside the register.

Round and round and round he went, learning nothing that Leland Dawson hadn't already discovered. People talked to Leland, he told himself, because Leland had arrived while the shock was new and people were still trying out different versions of the story. But that time had passed; the story had hardened into the official line: The dead sheriff and justice served, then betrayed, and finally, rightfully, carried out by a faceless group of outraged citizens. Deeply regrettable but unavoidable. A necessary evil. A dozen times a day he heard those opinions.

Round and round. There were good people here, Leland said, and Barrett found them too. One morning he sat in a lawyer's office near the courthouse as the man peered out the window and motioned him to stay out of sight while a few men from the depot strolled by outside. "I'd be shot through the window," he said, "if any of them saw me talking to you."

That afternoon on Laurens Street a woman beckoned him into a dark, stifling shop crammed with chairs and couches in every stage of breakdown and repair. Her advice was delivered around a mouthful of straight pins as she tucked and pinned heavy gold brocade onto a divan: "Don't go meddling in it. I'm telling you if they keep stirring it up, there will be more. And there isn't any use trying to get the straight of it. It's so crooked nobody will ever get it straight."

"In what way crooked?" he asked, and for an answer got more tugging and tucking and pinning. He felt foolish now, remembering how he'd stepped down from the train like an avenging angel come to bring justice to the dead. Now he felt more kinship with the dull yellow mule that turned the sorghum press in the vacant lot behind the lumberyard. On his way back to the hotel at the end of every day, he stopped to pat the animal on its thick plank of a nose. "Keep up the good work, pal," he said. At least the mule had syrup to show for its endless circling. At the end of most days he returned to his room with blank pages in his notebook and a telegram from his editor, Bayard Swope, waiting at the desk. "What news?" the latest read, an ominous brevity.

The Aiken County courthouse was brick, two stories tall, with a palmetto tree on either side of the entrance and a second-story balcony with a wide railing just made for a demagogue to pound, the way Pitchfork Ben Tillman had done while he proclaimed the white man's right to lynch the black man, the black woman too, if it came to that, to kill every last one of them if that's what it took to keep the white man in his rightful place on top of the heap.

Lying on his hotel bed one night with a drink balanced on his chest, letting the fan move warm air around the room—even in November the days were sometimes warm and humid, and his room stayed stuffy—he remembered the cool of the reading room at the New York Public Library, the long polished tables, the shaded lamps. He'd gone there to look up Ben Tillman's 1900 speech before the U.S. Senate in the *Congressional Record*. Tillman's logic was ferocious: He blamed the violence used to bring down South Carolina's Reconstruction government on the hotheadedness of blacks and the efforts of Republicans to put white necks under black heels. "We were sorry we had the necessity forced upon us," Tillman testified, "but we could not help it, and as white men we are not sorry for it, and we do not propose to apologize for anything we have done in connection with it." Why, he wondered now, were the evils here always necessary evils?

He remembered the shock of looking up from Tillman's words and finding creamy clouds and blue sky on the vaulted ceiling. The sky there had a heavenly cast, as though the pursuit of knowledge going on below was something holy, as though knowledge really were the greatest power. He'd believed that once, but now he understood that the idea was an illusion, a trompe l'oeil, like painted clouds and sky on a ceiling. Now he leaned more toward Tillman's logic: Power is power, and power is gained and kept by force and intimidation, by deceit and brutality. Power rests, always, with the man or men whose boots are most firmly planted on the necks of others.

Then one night as he brooded in his room, someone knocked. He opened the door to find Zeke in the hall, holding a cardboard box of laundry and smiling, as usual, at some private joke. "Come in, Zeke," he said, as usual, and as usual Zeke shook his head.

"No, sir, Mr. Barrett," he said. He set the box down on the threshold and nudged it into the room with his foot. "Mind those shirts, captain," he said over his shoulder as he clattered away down the stairs.

Under the stack of starched and ironed shirts, Barrett found a jar of whiskey. He held it up to the light, and for the first time since he'd gotten to town, he felt hopeful.

The next day more hope arrived. Just after noon a blue touring car appeared on Laurens, drove up one side of the street as slowly as a hearse, and turned onto Park Avenue, where it traveled three blocks at the same contemplative pace until it reached the courthouse and angled into a parking place out front. All along the route people stopped and turned and watched the car and its driver, a little man with a patch over one eye, sitting low behind the wheel.

Barrett was standing outside Holley Hardware when the car went by, and he cut through two vacant lots and sprinted across Park Avenue to beat the car to the courthouse so that he could be the first to shake hands with the man in the tweed suit who slid out from behind the wheel. "J. P. Gibson?" he said. He'd heard that Governor Arthur McCormick's investigator was en route at last, now that Barrett's badgering presence and the stories that appeared in almost every edition of the *State* and the *Charleston News and Courier* had made it too embarrassing for the governor to ignore what he called "the situation" down in Aiken.

The man's uncovered eye looked back, a feral shade of golden amber. His hand was pudgy and soft, but his grip was strong, and he held on as he leaned toward Barrett as though he had a secret to tell. "Correct," he said. The word seemed fired from him, and the force of it lifted him onto the balls of his feet then set him down again.

In New York men like J. P. Gibson were his allies: private eyes, house dicks, and police detectives, bodyguards and men who stood at the speakeasy doors; they were skillful with a blackjack, indifferent to fear, some of them veterans like himself. Barrett was so happy he whistled all the way from the courthouse to the depot, where he wired Swope: "Dam cracks. Hoping for flood. More to follow."

He waited two days before he went to see the sheriff again, allowing enough time for J. P. Gibson to rattle the lawman's chain, allowing him time to think through his own strategy. The jail was situated in back of the courthouse, surrounded by a high stone wall. He went in through a gate at one end of the wall, crossed the sandy yard, whistling, and stepped up onto the limestone stoop. The sheriff's back was to the door; he and the jailer, Robert Bates, sat across from each other at a table in mid-room, reading newspapers. When he knocked, the sheriff didn't turn.

"Come on in the house, Mr. Barrett," he said, sounding bored.

"How'd you guess?" Barrett stepped inside and waited for his eyes to adjust. The only light came from one bare bulb hanging by a frayed cord.

"It's my job to know who's coming up behind me," the sheriff said. "I know your walk and your whistle and your knock."

"Of course you do," he said. This morning Zeke had told him that the sheriff was a veteran too, and that made him a different kind of adversary, one who grasped the logic of survival as well as he did: If it comes down to me or you, it's going to be me. The sheriff stood up from the table and turned around. Barrett had never seen gravity so hard at work on a living man. His eyes, mouth, the flesh of his face itself, all trended south. He wore a black suit coat and dark trousers, a shirt with a tight, narrow collar band buttoned all the way up to his chin, round eyeglasses.

"Look who's here, Robert," the sheriff said out of the corner of his mouth. "This Yankee reporter can't get enough of us. I'd shake your hand," he said, holding up two bundles of bandages, "but I won't."

Robert Bates snickered, shrugged, hunched lower over his paper.

"Robert, go see that those prisoners get fed," the sheriff said without shifting his eyes from Barrett's face.

When Robert was gone, the sheriff looked somber, as though he had weighty news to tell. "I sent my jailer away so we can talk in private," he said. "I'm going to tell you something, Mr. Barrett, and I want you to write this down." He watched like a hungry man eyeing food as Barrett retrieved notebook and pencil from his jacket pocket and laid them on the table. "You know," he said, "when a man has been trying to administer the law the best way he can and them dirty political dogs say things, it's tough, I can tell you. All the time I've been sheriff, I've been giving the bootleggers hell, and now they're trying to drive me out. But I haven't the blood of them Longs on my hands. I wouldn't do a thing like that. I'm going to heaven; nobody's going to meet me in hell. No sir."

He looked at the notebook, but Barrett let it lie. "Did you tell that to Mr. Gibson?" Barrett said.

"I haven't had the opportunity yet, but I sure-bud plan to." When Barrett still didn't make a move toward his notebook, the sheriff trudged on. "I have something to show you," he said, and he crossed heavily to the rolltop desk next to the window and pawed out a few typewritten pages, clapped them between his bandages, and slid them down onto the table in front of Barrett. "My sworn testimony to the coroner's jury," he said. "Go on, read it out loud."

Barrett got out his glasses and slipped the wire stem over one ear, then the other. He cleared his throat. "I got to the jail, and fifteen or twenty men I guess were in front. I got on the steps there, and I said, 'Men there is nobody in Aiken County that has been hurt worse over Sheriff Glover's death than I am, but I am the sheriff now, and sworn to protect these prisoners, and I am neither scared of hell or heaven, and the first man that tries to go in this jail is going away from here tonight.'"

Barrett read the rest quickly, the facts so familiar he could have written the affidavit himself. Another version of the official story. The sheriff dispersed the crowd, but when he turned his back, they swarmed into the jail like a flock of blackbirds and overpowered him and Robert Bates. The electric lights were out, and it was dark in the jail, confusion and darkness on every hand.

They tied him and Robert up back in the kitchen and dragged the Longs from their cells. By the time the sheriff freed himself and found his gun, figured out where they'd gone, and raced after them out the Columbia Highway, found the turnoff and made his way up the edge of that field into the piney grove, the three of them were dead. All that was left for him to do was to beat out the fire in Bessie Long's dress. "Et cetera, et cetera," Barrett said, setting the paper down on the table.

"That there is the God's honest truth," the sheriff said, holding up his hands again.

Barrett shrugged. The notebook stayed closed. "How are those hands healing?" he asked.

The sheriff studied them, back and front. "Coming along," he said. "They're starting to itch, and Dr. Hastings tells me that's a good sign."

"Dr. Hastings, the coroner's physician? He takes good care of you, does he?"

"He's a doctor," the sheriff said. "That's his job."

"And you're the sheriff."

"Now who do you suppose has been spreading *that* rumor about me?" he said.

"It's all over town," Barrett said. The sheriff's name was at the top of Leland's list. Barrett wanted him to know he knew that.

The sheriff wanted him to know something too. He settled his bandaged hands on his belly, looked up with his sharp green eyes. "You and Mr. Gibson have a pleasant outing with the Rainey girl yesterday, down there in the valley with old James Moseley?"

"You tell me."

"All right. You did."

Barrett said nothing, trying to regain the high ground. He'd hoped to be the one to spring the news about the girl's affidavit. She'd been a prisoner in the jail on the night the Longs were killed. Gibson hadn't wanted to let Barrett go with them—so much for allies—but he'd talked his way into the car, and he and Gibson and the Rainey girl had driven down to Graniteville to swear her affidavit in front of Moseley, the justice of the peace. They'd avoided the Augusta Highway, found their way down to Graniteville along the hard clay back roads. The two men in the front and the girl in the back, a tired-looking girl with wary eyes, a dark shingle of hair, a necklace of puckered gold berries on a dirty string around her neck. "Chainy-berries," she called them when he asked, then looked at him as though she'd never seen anything like him before.

"You being a stranger and all, there's a few things about old Moseley that you need to put in your hopper," the sheriff said. "I don't know what he's got against me, but he's always had imaginings. He told me once he thinks he's the reincarnation of some general from three thousand years ago. Him and that Charlie George down at the Graniteville train station, they both have it in for me."

"He said the same about you," Barrett said. "That you have it in for him, I mean. Some Klan business from way back when?" Moseley protected himself from his imaginings with loaded guns. A shotgun leaned against a doorjamb, a pistol on a table. Moseley himself wore a .45 in a holster, and his three sons each carried a revolver. He'd watched them through the window of Moseley's stuffy office, patrolling the yard while his wife served them iced tea from a pitcher on a tray.

"Ah, hell," he said. "Like I said, he's always had imaginings."

"The Rainey girl said you gave her a pair of shoes when you let her out of jail," Barrett said.

"The poor sorry thing didn't have any," he said. "All's I'm saying is that there's things you should know about that little old girl that it's not Christian of me to divulge, and I wouldn't, if it wasn't my duty and you a stranger here and unfamiliar with a lot of things." He was a deacon in the Baptist church down in Graniteville. A God-fearing, Bible-reading man, his pastor said.

"Shoot," Barrett said, and for a second the sheriff's face lit up the way a match flares in a dark room. Don't I wish?

"You ask any law-abiding citizen in this county about that bunch, you'll get you an earful. To start with, her family's all bootleggers," he said. He'd known her people out in the Ellenton section for longer than he cared to remember, and the whole time he'd been sheriff, he'd been slapping them in jail for one thing or another, liquor mostly, which they all made and sold and drank. Ella was in jail in the first place because she'd tried to run away from a car full of gallon jugs of whiskey and beer that he'd stopped one night on the Aiken-Augusta highway.

Now Barrett opened his notebook, thumbed back through a few pages. "She said her father was a constable in Ellenton," he said.

The sheriff laughed, braced his hands on his knees, and went on laughing. "Did she say that? I guess the old loony spent so many days in the custody of lawmen, he started to believe he was one." That was how it went, the sheriff said, until one day, lo and behold, the old man turned up with a bullet through his head out in the piney woods behind the family shack where his daughter always went to whelp her young.

Barrett flipped through more pages in his notebook. "Just give me a minute," he said. "She said she heard your voice at the jail that night. Said you came up the stairs—here it is—'talking and laughing.'"

Everything in the sheriff's face stopped working at once, as though a gear had jammed in some good-humored machine. "Now look here," he said. "I don't know why she's telling dirty lies about me, but now that she is, I'm going to have to go look into it." He stood up from the table and crossed the room like someone excused from the witness stand, snatched his hat off a nail driven into the wall beside the door. "Why don't you take your notebook," he waved one bandaged hand in Barrett's direction, "and do some digging of your own. Instead of listening to whores and liars, why don't you go up to Laurens Street and call on the gentlemen in their offices? Ask them whose voices they heard that night. Go ask your friend Aimar. That's all I have to say at this time."

"One more question, sheriff. "Where did you serve?"

"St. Mihiel," he said, without turning. "And then the Meuse-Argonne. And I wouldn't try and use that against me if I were you."

"I was at Château Thierry," Barrett said. "And Château des Dames."

"Then you'd think we'd still be on the same side of things," the sheriff said as he shoved open the screen door so hard it banged against the front wall of the jail.

41

Back in his room Barrett wrote in his notebook and drank a glass of the whiskey Zeke had brought. It was strong and lively, with a bite, a burn, and when that glass was empty, he poured and drank another. It was three minutes to six when he arrived at Howard Aimar's office. The sun had dropped behind the buildings, and the gold letters on the glass door had gone dull. A cold peach light flooded the sky, and up and down Laurens Street the striped awnings were being rolled up for the night. At the end of the block the last trolley turned the corner and was gone.

A bell tinkled as he opened the door. The view from the front counter was what you'd see through the wrong end of a pair of field glasses: A man at a desk at the far end of a long, dim tunnel. A neat and natty young man in a gray pinstriped suit and rimless glasses, an old man's despair rounding his shoulders. Barrett often made snap judgments, but he didn't spare himself. "Body and imagination spurred by Dionysian longings, checked by Puritan steel," he wrote in the character assessment he drew up, after the war. "Result: much bucking and rearing, but no ground covered." He did not lack sympathy for this man and his life. If he'd gone home to New Bedford, he'd be sitting in an office like this on the mezzanine overlooking the weave room at his father's mill. But he was done with carrying out the plans and wishes of others.

"We close at six, sir," Howard Aimar said without looking up from his papers. Barrett walked through the swinging gate beside the front counter anyway. "I'll just take a second of your time," he said. Another lesson learned in France: nothing to be gained by hanging back. If a bullet has your name on it, hesitating won't keep it from finding you.

As Barrett walked toward him, Howard squared the stack of papers, straightened the line of fountain pens on the desk. "Mr. Barrett," he said. "May I help you?"

Barrett was used to the formality now; it was the way they let you know you'd never get close enough to merit a first name. "Mind if I get a squint," he said, nodding at the picture over Howard's desk.

"Help yourself."

Up close he saw cannon fire and sabers flashing through smoke and dust, a churning chaos of red and blue uniforms, dying horses and pale dead men, sunlight spread like a blessing over the heroes and their blood. "That was the moment," Barrett said, and Howard Aimar looked puzzled.

"The end of Napoleon," he said. "It's rare when one moment in one battle makes all the difference. Didn't happen in my war," he said. Then, to stop that thought from picking up speed, he said, "How'd you come by the picture?"

It was a story Howard Aimar seemed relieved to tell. It had hung over his father's desk in the pharmacy in Augusta, he said, and now it hung over his own, and he hoped that one day it would hang over his son's desk, and his son's and his son's. In his time here Barrett had noticed that much stock was placed on handing down and passing on, on loyalty and honor and keeping it in the family. They were bound to each other in so many ways that sorting out the connections would be like trying to untangle the root system in the ground beneath an ancient forest. Tangled, the upholsterer's wife should have said, not crooked.

A small black crucifix with a silver Christ hung on the wall under the picture of Waterloo. "You're Catholic," Barrett said.

"I am."

"Did I see you at the depot this morning?"

"Could be," he said. "My wife likes me to pick up the *State;* she keeps up with women's club doings and the like."

"I have met your wife."

"So she tells me." Aimar glanced at the wall clock with the slowly swinging pendulum, and when it began to strike six, he stood and patted his pockets, looking distracted.

"I'll let you go home to your dinner," Barrett said.

"Dinner is the midday meal, Mr. Barrett. The evening meal is called supper."

"You've saved me from further embarrassment."

"Happy to oblige." Howard switched off the desk lamp, put on a good gray topcoat, a soft gray hat. "What can I do for you, Mr. Barrett, in the few minutes remaining to us?"

The unexpected kindness of the man's tone unnerved him. Invite me to whatever you call the evening meal, he didn't say. Have a drink with me. "The sheriff says I should go up and down Laurens Street and ask every man where he was that night, what he saw and what he knows. So I thought I'd start with you." Remember his face, Barrett told himself. The startled face of a man in a dark room at the instant a light snaps on.

5

Howard Aimar

June 1943

H E WAITS BEHIND the privet hedge at the bottom of the yard behind the house, hoping that Libba remembered to oil the squeaky hinges on the back screen door. He's been here since two forty-five, the chosen time, but now it's three, and still she has not come. He studies the window of her second-floor bedroom, and when he cannot look any longer—because no one could be awake in a house so dark and still, because she could have been caught or changed her mind—he watches the pale sliver of new moon whose faintness had caused them to choose this night to run away and get married. He watches the moon, and when he looks toward the house again, Libba is running down the yard. Her legs flash white across the dark grass; the suitcase she carries is weightless. He steps out from behind the hedge. "Over here, my heart," he whispers.

Someone sits on the bed, pulling the sheet tight across his chest and thighs. *Are we going now?* he tries to say, but water trickles into his mouth and down his throat, and he knows by the path the water takes that Libba is pouring it. She carries the map of his body; she knows the way down his throat and into his belly and on, to his cock and his balls. He has never said those words to her, to anyone. The man who made love to his wife in the dark did not know those words, but the man he is becoming does. That man speaks, and she turns to him, opens her robe.

"There's that smile," Libba says, from somewhere above him. "You just needed some water, didn't you, sweetheart?"

The water trickling down his throat tastes like it has flowed from the kitchen tap at home. Even on the hottest summer days, the spigot there runs cool; the water tastes clean and bright and smells faintly of iron and stone, like the depths of the earth must smell. He will drink some of it soon, as he always does when he comes home after being away. Any day now he will run up the back steps and go into his house through the kitchen door. He will walk over to the sink, wrench the tap, fill his cupped hands, and drink and drink. "Use a glass, Howard," Libba always said. "Don't drink like a field hand."

It would be like Libba to bring him water from his own house. A mason jar of it held on her lap while Cecile drives them to the hospital. She is a genius at matching the cure to the disease, the gift to the need or desire. "Swallow, Howard," she says, but his throat refuses, and a man says, "That's enough." The water stops wandering down his throat, but before Libba's weight leaves the bed, he's thirsty again. He opens his mouth like a baby bird, but nothing comes.

Lewis's daughter is not like her grandmother or his own daughter either. It would not occur to her that he might be thirsty. She's like her father: agreeable one minute and so obstinate the next that it sometimes took a few licks with the belt to make Lewis mind. She has Lewis's wariness too, a look that says that at any moment she expects to have to fight for what she wants. But he can't take a belt to this one; he cannot lift his arms.

Did you tell Mr. Barrett that what happened to the Longs was unforgivable? she says.

No, no, no.

Isn't this you? she says, holding up a creased and yellowed newspaper clipping. "*In the downtown office of a prominent local businessman with ties to one of the town's oldest families, this correspondent was told that while what happened to the Longs was unforgivable, it was the work of a very small group of men, and this correspondent was treating it as if everyone in town was involved. 'That's what people resent,' said this gentleman, and as the six o'clock hour chimed, he brushed off his good gray fedora and settled it on his head.*

'But the identities of that very small group of men are well-known to a much larger group, so the question remains, who were those men?' this correspondent asked.

'Isn't that what we would all like to know?' he answered. But when pressed to name the unforgivable—the shotgun held under Albert's jaw? the bullet fired point-blank into Dempsey's heart? the pistol at Bessie Long's head? the burning dress? the common grave? the silence that cloaks the guilty?—he had no answer.'"

He hates the way she reads, impartial as a judge. It fills him with despair to see that everything he would have burned has come into her possession. He despises every one of the words she's just read, especially *unforgivable*. Hearing it again, he's reminded of what he'd meant, what he still means. A wrong that cannot be righted, that exists forever beyond the reach of forgiveness. A wrong that stained and drowned the soul, like the sin in Libba's favorite hymn:

> I was sinking deep in sin
> Far from the peaceful shore.
> Very deeply stained within
> Sinking to rise no more.

"You have no proof," he says. "You have no right."

I'm your flesh and blood, she says. *This is my story too.*

"Libba," he shouts. "Water."

But instead of Libba, he gets Cecile fussing with his pillow. He gets Lewis's daughter, holding a photograph up to his face like a mirror. *Look,* she says. *Be still.* He smiles to feel that the girl has a heart after all, to see the man he was and will be again. This was Libba's favorite picture of him: A man of substance in a double-breasted suit sitting easily in a chair with his legs crossed, a pair of black-and-white shoes on his feet, a cigarette held loosely between two fingers. His light hair is combed back from a high forehead, and he has strong lips and bold features, determined eyes behind rimless glasses. Libba made the appointment with the photographer. She brushed his suit and polished his shoes.

At the studio she ducked under the black cloth that the photographer held up for her, studied her husband's image floating upside down on the ground glass. "Look proud of yourself, Howard," she said. He'd straightened the crease of his trousers, done his best. She'd mounted the picture in a handsome black frame edged with sterling silver filigree and hung it in the hall; every week Minnie polished that silver. But he'd rather not remember Minnie or Zeke. He'd banished them from his thoughts years ago, and he does not appreciate their showing up now.

Grandmother told me that you ruined those shoes by wearing them out dove hunting, says Lewis's daughter. *Said she found them in a croker sack down in the cellar. Every time she looked at this picture, she told that story.*

He jerks the way you do when you wake from a dream of falling just before you hit the ground. Of course Libba had told the girl that story. Never could keep anything to herself, garrulous as the mockingbird in the cedar tree outside his window, telling the grandchildren about him in order to keep his image flickering in their minds. He can tell that Lewis's daughter wants to believe that story about the shoes. She looks eager and hopeful, the way her father looked, waiting for the answer after asking for something. "Yes," he says. "It's true that Libba told the dove field story."

But how did the picture come into this child's possession? Libba would not have given it to her. "Are you a thief?" he says.

Of course not, she says. *My father gave it to me after grandmother . . . ,* but he doesn't hear the rest.

"Where is my wife?" he roars. "My house? My son? The pictures in my hallway?" He sees that he has frightened her, and he is not sorry. She deserves to be frightened for forcing him to remember things that are best forgotten, asking him questions that he answered seventeen years ago, bringing back the sorrow and draining his strength.

He feels hands on his arms, another blanket thrown over him. Libba's frightened voice comes to him through heavy cloth. "Can't you give him something?" she says. "Can't someone help him?"

Lewis's daughter holds up another photograph, and the roaring stops. "Ah," he says, looking at his Libba smile at him from the greenhouse door at dusk, her body outlined by lantern light, a few strands of hair straggling out of a soft bun. "Her lamp does not go out at night," he whispers, and the curious grandchild leans close to hear more. Her hand rests lightly on his arm.

"She loved proverbs," he says. "She had one for every occasion. 'A soft voice turneth away wrath,' she'd say. 'A good wife is more precious than jewels. The heart of her husband trusts in her, and he will have no lack of gain.'

"I built that greenhouse for her the year that Lewis was born. Dr. Hastings didn't buy a single pane of glass." When he sees that she likes this story, he goes on. He tells her about kneeling on the ground with the sun on his back, smoothing mortar along the bricks of the foundation wall. Libba was so pregnant with Lewis she couldn't stand up for long, so he brought out a chair from the kitchen so she could sit and watch him work.

She was waiting at that same door the evening he came home after saying too much to Curtis N. R. Barrett, and he'd gone in gratefully, out of the low gray winter twilight into the lantern light, into the warm, moist, earth-smelling air, into her arms.

"She was dividing Dutch iris roots," he says. She must have figured he'd come there to help. "'Pick up a clump and flex it,' she said to me. 'You're looking for the compliant junctures.'" He flexed a complicated clot of tubers, sliced through the thickest part.

"Guess who came to see me today?" he said.

"Who?"

"Mr. Curtis N. R. Barrett."

"Oh?"

"I'm not the only one he visited," he said, so she'd understand. "He's talking to everybody in town about those killings."

"Well, what could you tell him, Howard, when you weren't there?" She was faster than he at dividing the root clumps, faster and more precise, and remembering her skill, her sureness, remembering the two of them together that night, is making him feel stronger, the way the water she gave him earlier did.

49

"I said it was a terrible thing, a very regrettable affair. 'But some-times it takes a violent storm to clear the air,' I said. And that is exactly what that night was. A violent storm that only the Almighty could have stilled, a cataclysm beyond the reach of human judgment or con-trol."

6

Minnie Settles

November 1926

S HE STOOD AT the sink with her hands in the soapy water and watched discreetly as Libba parted the short yellow curtains and looked out. Spying on her husband again, checking to see whether he'd left for work or if he was walking back to the house for a clean handkerchief and another minute in her arms, the way he did nearly every weekday morning now.

This morning he must have made it out of the driveway because Libba dropped the curtain and turned away. Minnie looked down at the water but not fast enough to miss the way Libba stared around her own kitchen like she didn't know the place. She had no time for sympathy. In less than three hours the Little Garden Club would arrive for their last meeting before the flower show, and she had a mile-long list of chores to finish. The day began when work began, and it ended when work was finished. She'd been idling in the kitchen long enough, waiting for Mr. Aimar to go; now it was time to get busy, the way she'd done all her life.

By the time she was old enough to work, they were farming cotton on shares for Mr. Gregorie, but she'd heard stories. Back in slavery times her mother's family had worked in rice on Tomotley Plantation, down in Beaufort County. "Girl," her mother always said, "that was toil the likes of which you better hope you never have to bend your back to." Vast, flooded fields and labor endless as the tide that pushed the river over the dikes and into the rice. They and their kin had fled those fields early in the Civil War, right after the Union army occupied that part of the coast.

As a child in Aiken County, she'd followed her parents and her brother up and down the rows of Mr. Gregorie's fields, filled her sack with cotton and dragged it to the scale, watched to make sure that the fat man tending the scale wrote down the correct weight next to her name. "No bigger than a minute," he said. "And look at her go." After her father died, her mother moved them into Aiken, sent Minnie to the Schofield School. She graduated with a housekeeping certificate on top of a general high school diploma, worked around town for a few other families before the Aimars hired her. Now her work was here. Laundry on Monday and mending on Tuesday. On Wednesday she polished the silver, cleaned the pantry and the icebox. On Thursdays she cleaned the living room, the hall and the stairs, the dining room, and the long, narrow closet in the hall where the coats and hats and overshoes were kept. Fridays she tackled the bedrooms and bathroom. Saturdays she tidied closets, scrubbed the kitchen and the icebox, again. Every day but Sunday she cooked and served three meals. Last thing every night she brushed Libba's hair while they planned the next day's meals and errands.

She was famous all over town for her skill at the washtub and iron-ing board and mangle. She had a callus on her pointer finger from licking the tip and touching it to a hot iron. "Working her magic," Libba called Minnie's way with a shirt, a blouse, a fine linen tablecloth, or one of the new corsets with the dangling stocking clips. The Aimars kept a washing machine on the back porch of the house, where she washed the bedsheets and dishtowels and the like. They had a mangle in the cellar, where she pressed the table linens. She was happy to use the machines for those chores, but for the fine laundry she still favored a copper boiler, an iron kettle, her own brew of bluing and soap flakes and bleach mixed into boiling water.

"My good right hand," Libba called her. "My dear Minnie. My treasure." Libba's friends brought their laundry to Minnie, and she was their treasure too. She'd heard herself called every pretty name in the book, and not one of them worth the breath it took to say it if they ever turned against her. The word going around was that Bessie Long had been taken to the killing ground in her shift, denied even the minor dignity of clothing.

Libba walked to the canary's cage, lifted off the canvas cover, and dropped it into the drawer where it was kept. "All right, Louie, rise and shine," she said, and the bird hopped up onto his perch and started singing. Lately the cover stayed on the birdcage until Howard left for the office because Louie's shrill singing, the clicking of his beak on the cuttlebone, made Howard nervous. It looked like everything unsettled Mr. Aimar now, Libba had told Minnie, and her husband's jumpiness, the wincing, hunted look that often appeared in his eyes, made her remember that the obituary had listed the cause of death of Mr. Aimar's father as "nervous prostration." Not even her own doctor father had been able to explain to her satisfaction what that meant, only that it was dire, unpredictable, and likely inherited. That was why the house had to be kept calm and quiet until he left for work. Once he was gone, Minnie could bang her pots and pans, Louie could sing his heart out, and Little Mister could clomp down the stairs, eat the yolk out of the middle of a fried egg, and ride off to school in Zeke's wagon. They could all get on with the day.

Libba sat down at the small white table beside the pantry door with her hands folded tightly on the tabletop. She wore a plain white blouse and a dark-blue skirt, and her hair was pinned up on top of her head. She always dressed for breakfast, wouldn't dream of coming to the table in her bathrobe. "Looking slovenly," she called it, and she wouldn't have it.

"Oh, Lord, Minnie," she said. "What are we going to do about my husband?"

She'd been dreading this invitation to sit and talk, the way they'd done nearly every morning for the ten years she'd been working here. The two of them sitting down for a few minutes before they both got on with the day, puzzling out what to do about Little Mister's bed-wetting or Libba's friend Olivia, who couldn't seem to keep it straight what day she needed to pick up her laundry.

"You'll think of something, Miz Libba," she said over her shoulder, careful to keep the *we* out of it. Because there was no *we* anymore, not since the morning of the night the Longs were killed, when she'd heard a car door slam and seen Mr. Aimar hurry across the driveway to the spigot outside the greenhouse, where he washed one shoe, then the other, under the running water. Now those shoes were up in this house, under the same roof with them. Yesterday afternoon she'd come across Libba carrying a croker sack into the hall closet. "Oh, Minnie," she said. "You startled me." She held up the sack, told some story about how Mr. Aimar had worn his good shoes out dove hunting. "Can you imagine?" she said.

By ten o'clock a dozen thin white china cups and saucers were arranged on a linen cloth on the freshly polished silver tray. In the front room the fire was laid, chairs carried in from the dining room. She'd changed into a black taffeta uniform and a clean white apron, pinned the stiff white cap on her head, and though she'd dusted the front room yesterday, she dusted it again. She brushed the feather duster over the frame of the picture of the high-and-mighty man on his high-and-mighty horse, over the lampshades and along the mirror over the mantel, over the clock and the two porcelain spaniels that guarded it. She even got down on her hands and knees and dusted the claw feet on the marble top table in front of the settee; she'd been raised to do a good job, no matter what.

Before she went upstairs to change, Libba stood in the doorway and admired the front room. She said she hoped the ladies would appreciate the way the yellow, bronze, and red in the arrangement of fall daisies and autumn leaves on the mantel picked up the colors in the wallpaper. She hoped her attention to detail, the care she'd taken with the room, would inspire them to strive for greater heights. Next to her husband, her son, and her church, Libba loved the Aiken Flower Show best. Her mother had started it, and in the six years since her mother passed and she was elected president of the Little Garden Club, she'd been working to make the show better every year. She was determined to make this year's edition perfect to the last detail, nothing overlooked or forgotten or sloughed off or haphazardly done. Every *i* dotted, every *t* crossed, she said, in memory of her mother and her brother killed in the war and for the sake of her husband and the town she loved that had lately been so maligned.

But when the ladies started arriving, no one seemed to notice the front room. In the foyer the younger ones squeezed hands and kissed cheeks. They all dressed like Libba, in long skinny dresses with shiny stockings and high-heeled shoes, and they turned in front of each other, showing off. A few wore big curls pasted to each cheek. The old ones still dressed in long dark skirts and plain white blouses, as they'd done throughout the war, as if they hadn't heard that it was over. As soon as she'd taken their wraps and they were all settled in the front room on the sofa and the dining room chairs, Minnie served the pound cake and poured the coffee and listened to them talk and whisper among themselves about everything *but* the room that Libba had made so welcoming for them.

Meanwhile, Libba sat there in her skinny plaid velvet dress with her ankles crossed, the cup and saucer balanced on one knee, pretending it didn't bother her that nobody had noticed how she'd decorated the room. She chatted to this one and that one, smiling at them like her smile was a prize they'd won, but Minnie could tell she was upset. The more bothered Libba got, the bigger and brighter she smiled. She was tempted to say something, the habit of loyalty as hard to break as any other. Maybe they'd forgive her for stepping out of line. "What do y'all ladies think about that pretty arrangement?" she'd like to say. Or: "You know, she had me make this lemon pound cake because one of you said it was her favorite."

Instead, she poured coffee and listened, fought back the temptation to answer a question or two herself. "Do we know for sure," asked old Miss Rosamond Phelps, "that the governor was sent a list of names?"

"Yes, ma'am, he was," Minnie didn't say. "Thanks to Mr. Leland Dawson. Honor his name."

Curtis N. R. Barrett came into the conversation too. His name was spoken with mockery and outrage. Finally, someone said, "What do you think, Libba?"

"What do I think?" she said, and she put a finger to her lips, pretending to mull it over. "Well, yesterday I was down at Hahn's, picking out potatoes for Sunday's au gratin, and he came in and walked right up to me. 'Mrs. Aimar,' he said, and I said, 'Mr. Barrett,' and I went right on sorting my potatoes." She had their attention now, Minnie's too; she went around the room with the coffeepot again. Zeke had told her about driving the man all over town, the errands he ran for him almost every day. "You stay clear of that whiskey mess," she'd told him, but from the way he cut his eyes away and mumbled into his shirt collar, she knew it was too late.

Libba said that she and this Mr. Barrett exchanged a few words about potatoes. She filled her sack and folded the top down and creased the fold, and then she said, "How do you like our little town, Mr. Barrett?" and he said it was very pleasant so far, though he doubted it would stay that way for long, where he was concerned.

That's when she'd seen her opening. "'Well, Mr. Barrett,' I said, 'my mother had a saying: Though a lie be swift, the truth overtakes it.'" She said she hoped the truth would overtake him soon, and he said he hoped so too.

"But what does he look like?" one of the younger ones asked.

"Handsome in a bland sort of way," Libba said, studying her fingernails. "Nothing to write home about." She waved a hand in front of her face like she was shooing a gnat, and the ladies all laughed, and the fresh air came in through the open windows. "Thank you, Minnie," they said. "Just half a cup, please, Minnie."

Didn't Mr. Eubanks, editor of the *Aiken Standard,* say it best, Libba asked, when he expressed his profound regret that this unfortunate community was made the scene of an inhuman horror? Minnie set the coffeepot back on the tray, the tray on the table nearest the door. She went to the fireplace and jabbed at the fire with the poker, sending a shower of sparks up the chimney, thinking of what Mr. N. R. Latham had to say about regret. The Mt. Hebron Baptist Church subscribed to his paper, the *Palmetto Leader.* She could quote chapter and verse of his opinion. "Those are not the kind of murders that law officers find out about," he wrote. "They only furnish the occasion for an expression of regret on the part of good citizens."

She'd better leave now, she thought, before she said something she'd be sorry for, and she went back and sat in the kitchen with her hands wound in her apron to keep them still. When she heard the mantel clock chime the quarter-hour, she went back to the front room and loaded the plates and cups and napkins onto the silver tray—"You're welcome, ladies, you're welcome"—and carried them to the kitchen, and no one was the wiser. She filled the sink with hot water, sprinkled in the soap flakes while Louie shrilled away. Mr. Aimar wasn't the only one whose nerves got worked by Louie's singing. She put her face up close to the cage. "Hush up, Louie," she said, and the bird fumbled a few notes then picked up the tune again.

It got quiet in the front room, and she pushed open the kitchen's swinging door and listened to see if she was needed. Then Libba's voice started. "Best Three White Chrysanthemums," she said. "Best Center-piece of Chrysanthemums." Minnie let the door swing shut, went back to the sink. "Let's us say them too, Louie," she said. "Best Three Yellow, Pink, Crimson Chrysanthemums," Minnie said, washing a cup and setting it on a dish towel on the drainboard. "Best Begonia in a Pot. Best Vase of Dahlias. Best Boston Fern, Asparagus Fern, Best Geranium in a Pot. Say *geranium,* Louie," she said, but the little bird just kept singing.

She washed faster, but it rushed back into her mind anyway, the picture that she'd seen when Libba had talked about the truth overtaking a lie. The idea of overtaking was what lingered and got mixed up with Louie's singing and the memory of seeing those three dead people.

Tweet, the undertaker's canary, had been singing its fool head off, too, when she and Annie Matthews walked into the room where the Longs were laid out. They were carrying the clothes the Daughters of Zion had collected: a navy blue dress for Bessie Long, pants and shirts for the boys. Right away Mr. Jackson stepped over and covered the birdcage, and then the room was quiet. Quiet and still and white. The windowpanes were painted white; the sink on the wall was white and the sheets he'd pulled over them; the whole room was white, except for the cotton sacks that had covered their bodies in the back of the truck that had carried them into town. Those were piled in one corner, at the end of a long smear of blood.

When Mr. Jackson drew back the sheet over Albert, Annie cried out, "Dear Jesus," and fled. Minnie had felt weak herself, and the undertaker had led her to a chair in one corner, made her sit, and handed her a funeral fan on a stick. After that she tried not to look at what Mr. Jackson was doing with the clothes they'd brought, but she saw enough to know that it would take more than clothes to make those people look content, the way the dead were supposed to look. Later, when she heard how they'd been carried out to Monetta in the back of a county truck and buried in a common grave, she knew she'd been right: No clothes ever sewed by a human hand could have decently covered the look of the fate they'd met.

"Hush, fool," she said to Louie, and she flicked a finger against his cage. The bird hopped sideways on the perch and went on singing. She opened the little wire door and stuck her finger inside, and he hopped onto it. Libba had taught him that trick, and now he sat on her finger, oblivious to how much she'd like to snap his neck, tell Libba (who would go all to pieces over that bird) that she'd left the kitchen for a minute and come back to find him dead.

When Libba rang the handbell, Minnie went back to the front room and handed out the ladies' wraps and saw them out the door, and when they were alone in the kitchen, Libba sat down at the table again. "Mr. Aimar is just not himself, Minnie," she said, as though they were picking up a conversation they'd dropped earlier. "That's what worries me," she said, turning her wedding band and the diamond engagement ring around and around. The lipstick had worn off her mouth, and her face looked thin and famished.

Who is he, then? Minnie didn't say. *Is he one of them who'd done what had been done to those three people? Or did he only watch while they were overtaken?*

Walking down to her house after the Aimar's supper dishes had been washed and dried and put away, she peered into shadows, startled at a flash of moonlight in a pane of greenhouse glass. "Just tired, that's all," she told herself. But it wasn't until she'd settled herself in the armchair on her own back porch and lit up an Old Gold cigarette that she felt out of danger. She blew a procession of perfect smoke rings, watched them march away into the dark, then looked where they'd gone: out over the dozing fires under the copper boiler and the laundry kettle in the sandy patch of ground just beyond the porch and on to her privy and the two long clotheslines held up by bamboo poles. Out past the clotheslines her garden was filled with puckered tomatoes on drooping plants, withered bean vines, and the woody spires of okra. It was quiet back there, so quiet she could hear the grasshoppers rustle in the dry grass between the garden rows and the thinning autumn songs of the crickets. Out there on her porch in the dark, she could almost believe that this was her own little house on her own piece of land.

She'd just dropped the cigarette butt into her skirt pocket when Zeke's wagon rumbled down the driveway. She heard the heavy thud of Princess's hooves, the clunk of the wooden brake dropping into its slot. The horse blew hard—*Amen, sister,* she thought—and then Zeke came clomping down the path beside the house. How could a tall, skinny boy walk as heavy as an ox? That was just one of the multiplying mysteries that vexed her about her son. He came around the corner, carrying a bundle of laundry tied in a sheet.

"Mama, why do you work so hard for everybody but yourself?" he said, dropping the bundle next to her chair.

With his hat pulled down and his chin jutted out like he was spoiling for a fight, he looked exactly like his father.

"Just used to it, I guess," she said. "And good evening to you too. What did you bring me?" she said, nudging the bundle with her foot.

"Some shirts. And the gentleman needs them back quick."

"I'm taking my leisure here, son," she said. He grumbled something she didn't hear. Just as well—she wasn't going to quarrel with Zeke tonight. Woman-trouble, no doubt, it always was with him. But every day she thanked God for him, for all he did for her and all he meant to her. Thanks to him, her roof did not leak, her firewood was split and stacked; she couldn't remember the last time she'd lifted anything heavy or missed church. Her church and Zeke were her family now. The rest of her blood kin were dead or gone north, who knew where?

"You can go on and get started clearing my garden, if you're looking for something to keep you out of trouble," she said. He clumped off the porch and out into the patch, yanked up a few tomato plants, poles and all, and tossed them out into the dark. She knew these signs; he'd always had a temper, and when it flared up, it burned whatever or whomever stood too close. His temper and his pride, the two hard edges of his character that she worried about all night sometimes. The last time she'd had a good taste of both was when he'd left the Schofield School the day he turned fifteen.

He'd been the biggest boy in the sixth grade class, tired of wearing the little blue cap that all the boys wore, bored with chair caning, resentful about working on the school farm. Why should he learn to be a field hand? he'd said; he didn't intend to be a tenant, ever. Then don't be, she'd said. Any colored businessman in town would have hired him. Ezra Jones had taken her aside after church one Sunday and said he'd be glad to hire Zeke at his tailor shop. The Ford brothers always needed an extra hand with what they were building. Everyone was always on the lookout for a smart, quick young man.

But that was where Zeke's pride came in, and pride could get you killed. A lot of things could get you killed, and that fact had recently become very clear again, as it seemed to do periodically. It was like a lesson they had to keep teaching you until it took root somewhere deep down inside you: Stay humble, stay quiet. But rather than work for anyone else, even one of their own, he'd drive his wagon around town and be at the beck and call of anyone who whistled; he'd sleep on a palette on the floor at Gregorie's cotton gin in exchange for running Mr. Gregorie's errands during the day and call that being his own boss. Worrying about Zeke used to keep her up a few nights a week; now it seemed that almost every night when she closed her eyes to sleep, the Longs' shattered bodies appeared, and the only way to keep them from coming was to lie awake all night.

It wasn't that you had to *be* humble, she'd told Zeke. You just had to *act* that way because you never knew when the same white man who'd laughed at your foolishness one day might decide on the next that he'd had enough of your mouth or the way you wore your hat, and before you knew what had happened, you might find yourself in the penitentiary in Columbia or cutting weeds with a sling blade along a county road in the heat of the day, if you could find yourself at all. "Mind those bean poles, son," she said. "Take them up and lean them over here against the back of the house. You know I carry them over from year to year."

He stomped along the rows. "Why do you keep all this damn mess out here once it's died back?" he said.

"Whose shirts are these?" she said, hoping to distract him.

He was working slower now, stripping the dead bean vines off the poles and stacking them in his arms, not tossing them off into the weeds in the dark where she'd have to go and hunt them up the next day. "Mr. Curtis N. R. Barrett," he said. "That newspaperman who's come down here to look into what happened."

She stood up from her chair. "Boy, don't you know there's nothing to be done for those people now," she said. "Nothing. And you know as well as I do that nobody's going to pay. Don't you read the papers?" He stopped in front of the porch, holding his bundle of sticks, watching her. "Well, I do," she said. "The Aiken paper says the many should not be blamed for the crimes of the few. Says this whole community's been made the scene of an inhuman horror." She'd quote Mr. N. R. Latham to him, but why waste her breath? "America has a peculiar system of law enforcement," Mr. Latham had written in his last editorial. "When one or two men commit a murder they can as a rule be found and arrested. But when a hundred or more engage in this pastime, it seems impossible to discover a thing about it. In other words, the greater the number engaged, the less is the chance of finding out who did it. There seems to be great safety in numbers."

"Just finish up out there, son," she said, waving her hand in the general direction of her garden. "I'm tired of your foolishness." She sat down suddenly, her heart running hard, and braced for what he'd say next.

But he turned and waded back out into the tomato patch. "You know you're exactly right, Mama," he said over his shoulder. "I guess what we better do is just let it lie." He was out in the bean rows now, swishing through the tall, dry grass. "Just some kind of necessary evil," he said. "Some kind of violent storm."

"Where you been listening to that kind of talk?" she said.

"Man whose clothes you got there told it to me, says he heard it from a prominent local businessman."

Fussing with Zeke made her late getting back up to the house, and by the time she made it, Libba was waiting at her dressing table with her hair unpinned and down around her shoulders, tapping the fancy hairbrush with her initials engraved on the silver back against her hand.

Brushing Libba's hair at night hadn't been on the list of duties when they'd hired her. Early on she'd started going up to Libba's dressing room every night to talk over the next day's meals and chores while Libba drew the brush through her hair a hundred times, until one night Minnie took it out of her hand, said, "Let me do that." The next night Libba handed her the brush, and now doing Libba's hair at night was one of her duties, like dusting or ironing or cooking, something she couldn't stop doing, even though she wanted to. But what would she say—"I can't be tending to your hair anymore, Miz Libba. Can't joke around with Mr. Aimar either or play hide-and-seek with Little Mister on a rainy afternoon like I'm family"?

She picked up the brush and pulled it through Libba's thick, dark hair. By the time she got to fifty strokes, they'd settled on stewed chicken for the next night's supper. Then Libba started to sigh and smooth the white dresser cloth. Finally, she looked up at Minnie in the mirror, one hand on her cheek. Her blue eyes were like searchlights. "You know, Minnie, I look forward to the day when this whole terrible business will be behind us," she said. "We all just have to do our best to make that happen." She gestured around the room as if the terrible business had happened right there.

"Yes, ma'am." She looked at the two of them in the mirror, Mrs. Aimar in her dressing gown and she in a white gauze blouse Libba had given her when it started to look worn, a hand-me-down with a row of small pearl buttons all the way up the high collar and satin stripes on the sleeves and bodice. *Let it pass.* Only an hour ago she'd given Zeke the same advice.

And then the hundred strokes were done, and she was standing outside the closet in the downstairs hall where she straightened the coats and hats and galoshes every week. She was opening the door, stepping inside. It was pitch-black dark in the closet, but she needed no light. The croker sack was behind the boots and shoes lined up under the coats on the back wall, and her hands found it easily. She'd been wrong to tell Zeke that nothing could be done. The old had no right to pass on their fears to the young like they were God's commandments struck in stone. She should have told him that as long as you had breath in your body, you could do something. You could reach behind those coats and shoes and boots and pick up that croker sack and carry it down the back steps and across the yard, holding it away to keep it from touching you, not knowing what you'd do when you opened it and saw what was in there. You could do all that without a thought about what came next, knowing that if Libba asked what became of those good shoes that Mr. Aimar had ruined in the dove field, you'd think of something. White people weren't the only ones who could look a person in the face and lie.

7

Aubrey Timmerman

November 1926

H E EASED THE black Ford in under the low limbs of the water oak that grew between the courthouse and the jail, killed the spark, climbed out. He unlocked the gate in the high stone wall, locked it behind him, and trudged across the bare yard. It had been a dry fall, but today was warm and muggy, the sun a blurred patch of light in a hazy sky. Not as hot and smothering as summer, of course, more like a memory of summer, but warm enough to bring a sweat. Closer to the jail he heard a clatter of pans from the kitchen, a few whistles from the barred windows on the second floor. As usual, the prisoners were watching, waiting for him to look up so they could joke with him, but he couldn't be bothered with their foolishness this morning. It was barely seven o'clock, but his bones already felt as heavy as they did at the end of a whole day's worth of trouble.

The words that weighed heaviest were the ones Curtis Barrett had written about the men who claimed they'd talked to the lynchers, before and after the crime. He'd like to talk to those men himself, ask why in hell they hadn't brought the sheriff what they knew instead of running their mouths to some New York reporter who'd hung flypaper all over town for them to blunder into. Barrett had come to the jail half a dozen times now, always with a new batch of questions:

On what grounds did you arrest Dempsey Long after the judge set him free?

Why didn't you stay at the jail the night of the killings? Didn't you think there was any danger?

Walk me through that night one more time. I'm a little unclear about the details.

Then Barrett would watch and wait for him to trip himself up, as though in the thick of all the shouting and flailing and stumbling around in the pitch-black dark that went on that night, he should have kept track of everything and everybody.

"Even a blind pig finds an acorn now and then," his mother always said, and sure enough, Barrett had found Jesse Finley, the lumberman, and published Finley's boast that he spoke for 90 percent of the people in town who were glad the Longs had been killed. All week Finley had been carrying the clipping in the pocket of his overalls, pulling it out to show to anyone who'd stand still long enough to listen to him read it, proof of what a big shot he was.

Personally, he had to reach back a long way to remember a time when a newspaper had said something good about him. He had to go all the way back to the story of how he'd been named sheriff right after Bud Glover died. They'd printed that one up under the masthead on the front page of the *Aiken Standard* and spread a big headline over the picture of him looking like the man the write-up said he was: the one who had no favorites, who followed the law as it was written.

His wife had cut the article out of the paper and stuck it in her Bible; he'd had her bring it to him this morning so he could read it again before he left for work. The paper had yellowed, but the story still held true. It told how, after the Longs killed Sheriff Glover, men from every corner of the state had vouched for Aubrey Timmerman to the governor. They'd spoken of his devotion to duty, his high regard for the things the average man does not understand, and his dedication to the law, which since it is the law he must preserve it. True then, and true now. He needed to pay Finley a call, inform him that the average man needed to understand when to keep his trap shut.

The phone was ringing as he stepped into the office, but before he answered, he turned the latest edition of the *Columbia Record* face down on the battered wooden desk. "Aubrey Timmerman here," he said, crisply. "State your business."

"Sheriff Timmerman, hold for the governor, please," a woman's voice said.

It wasn't unusual for the governor to phone. His Honor had called to congratulate him after his first big liquor raid got written up in the *Standard* and many times since, to talk over one piece of law enforcement business or another. Surely, this morning's call was to express outrage at the rank lie that Barrett's article had made of Timmerman's statement about being overpowered. From back in the kitchen he smelled biscuits; he felt hungry, and then he felt sorry for himself that he wouldn't be able to eat a few while they were still warm because he had to be on the phone, explaining God knows what to the governor again.

When Arthur McCormick came on the line, he was breathing hard, still winded, no doubt, from hauling his stout little self up all those steps in front of the statehouse. "You're up awful early, Your Honor," he said.

"Sheriff Timmerman," the governor said—his tone was not encouraging—"sounds like there's a whole lot of whispering going on down in your neck of the woods."

"Yes, sir, it does look that way," he said. He yanked open the long shallow desk drawer, looked at the gnawed pencil and the pad of yellow paper there, and felt sorry for himself again. Of course the governor had seen the latest headline in that New York paper: "South Carolina Whispers Names of Mob Killers." He'd heard from a reliable source in Columbia that McCormick sent a man down to the depot every night to meet the southbound train so he'd have the latest papers on his desk first thing every morning.

"Now look here," the governor said. "I want you—I *expect* you—to cooperate with my detective and show him every courtesy. And I am troubled by that girl's affidavit, sir, I'll not deny it."

So what he'd heard around town was true: yesterday J. P. Gibson had hustled back to Columbia carrying affidavits from the Rainey girl and a colored man named Martin, who'd been in the jail the night the Longs were killed.

The governor cleared his throat and began to read:

I got up from the bed and went to the door and looked out through the window in it toward the stairs. It was dark, and I couldn't see anything. I could hear men talking. I could not hear what was being said, but I recognized the voice of Sheriff Aubrey Timmerman. With him were four other men. They went to Bessie Long's cell. I recognized as one of the five men Robert Bates, the jailer, who had a black robe on and was carrying a lantern. He unlocked the door of Bessie Long's cell and then stepped around to a bathroom. Sheriff Aubrey Timmerman, who I recognized by his back and his voice, said something to Bessie Long, and she got up and started putting on her clothes. He told her it wasn't any use to dress; the sheriff just wanted to see her. She went to crying and asked him where was the sheriff. They brought her on, and when she got even with my cell door, she went to crying louder; she cried until she got even with the men's cage. Then she said, "Lord, I will never see him anymore." They told her to hush three times. I don't know who told her.

"There's things you should know about that girl, sir," he said, but the governor kept rumbling down his own track.

"This Barrett SOB has us by the short hairs," he said. The sheriff looked down at the dark wood floor, the way he would have done if he'd opened a door and found the governor compromised. The governor was a pious man, high up in the Methodist church; he chastised men for saying *damn* and *hell* in his presence. He had a favorite story, which Aubrey Timmerman had heard half a dozen times now, about Robert E. Lee reprimanding a Confederate officer for an off-color remark. "But, sir," the officer said. "There are no ladies present."

"No, sir, but there *are* gentlemen," Lee answered.

"I suppose you've seen that Wesley Barton mess too?" the governor said. He was breathing easier now.

"I'm looking at it as we speak," the sheriff answered, and he flipped over the *Record*. There on page 1 was what Mr. Barton, a South Carolina man, had written about his fellow citizens.

The serene confidence that sustained the mob leaders in the belief that they could get completely away with wholesale murder has been shattered under the cold scrutiny of the outside world that is now searching its dark corners. The "patriots" who led the mob through the open door of the county jail to play an improbable game of Blind Man's Buff in the darkened corridor where the stalwart sheriff and the jailer were so easily overpowered are not as sure of themselves as they were a month ago. Names were being whispered of organizers, ringleaders, participants, and witnesses who stood on the sidelines. They are beginning to be sensible of the fearful and rotten blight of lawlessness that must pervade Aiken County to have enabled it to muster so many human buzzards to such a feast. They are beginning to ask themselves if they have not been deluded with regard to the efficiency, heroism, and devotion to duty of their peace officers.

It never ceased to amaze him how newspaper people could take upright, decent words like *stalwart* or *patriots* or *peace officers* and make them stink to high heaven. So the governor was calling to agree with him that there is nothing worse than being betrayed by one of your own, to let him know that he would not have the good name and integrity of his peace officer undermined by innuendo or the affidavits of one whore girl and a colored criminal who hadn't had any more light to see by than anyone else that night. When he could get a word in edgewise, he'd also remind the governor that no one of any consequence had uttered a word against him.

"Yes, sir," the governor said. "A lot of whispering. What I'm trying to impress upon you, sheriff, is that we have to take this business seriously."

"I am well aware, Your Honor." Two of the governor's cousins were on Leland Dawson's list of ringleaders and perpetrators. "You have my word that I will assist Detective Gibson in his investigation by every means available to me."

"Fine, sir, see that you do," the governor says. "I don't intend to leave office under a cloud."

"No, sir," Aubrey Timmerman said, and then, without a word of encouragement or farewell, the governor hung up.

The sheriff sat at the wooden desk and read Wesley Barton's article again and then Barrett's latest screed. It made his jaw tense to hear himself sounding like a mealymouthed simpleton. "Why, I just felt sorry for that girl, that's all," Barrett had him saying. "And I don't even know Martin by name. I declare, I don't know why they got it in for me." He stared at the new pink flesh on the palms of his hands. Yesterday Dr. Hastings had unwound the last bandage, and now he could make a fist again without wincing, though the new pink skin felt tight, binding. He stared at his hands then picked up the gnawed pencil, smoothed down the top sheet on the pad of yellow paper in front of him. He'd best start sketching out what he was going to say when Gibson came to take his affidavit.

Gibson wore a black patch over one eye, and the other eye was small and cold, an unnerving shade of amber. Just looking at him rattled some people, but not him. He'd invite the man to take a seat in a chair directly across the desk from him, to show that he had nothing to hide. Doing anything with Gibson involved waiting while he fished a can of Prince Albert smoking tobacco and papers out of the pocket of his suit coat and set up shop on the desktop, so Aubrey would sit tight while the detective rolled and licked and sealed and tamped himself a smoke. His fat little fingers were surprisingly nimble. Then, once he'd scraped his match across the desk and lit up, brushed off his pad of paper, and licked the point of his pencil, they could begin. But no matter where the detective wanted to start, the sheriff was determined to start where *he* knew the story began.

Let's go back to the night of April 25, 1925, he would say, the night of the day that Bud was gunned down, because that was where the trail began that ended on the night of October 8, 1926, and to understand one, you had to grasp the other. On that April night a crowd had also come to take the Longs, he'd say, and Aubrey Timmerman had stood in the jailhouse door with Mack and Frank Bell, and together the three of them had faced down the mob. It was a big crowd too, he'd remind Gibson, come with torches and guns.

Standing there, he'd heard a roaring in his head, but when he looked down, he saw that the shotgun in his hands was rock steady, and that had been a surprise and a relief. His arm still hurt like the devil where Bessie Long had torn a chunk out of it that morning, and whenever he closed his eyes, pictures flashed through his head: Bud lying dead in the Long's yard, lying dead in his casket in the courthouse not ten yards from the jail, while his orphaned children drooped and clung to their mother and she asked everyone who came to pay respects what in God's name she was going to do now.

Yes, sir, he would say to Mr. J. P. Gibson, that night he'd been tempted, and he made no apologies for that, he'd been *strongly* tempted, to step aside and let the mob get what they'd come for, but that would have been a smirch on the memory of the man who'd helped Aubrey Timmerman become the man he was that night. Only a few years earlier Aubrey had been a conductor on the trolley that ran from Aiken down through Horse Creek Valley and over the river to Augusta and back. Bud's people were from the valley too, and when he rode the trolley home, they'd talk about their families and this and that.

Then one day Bud said he was looking to hire a couple more deputies and would Aubrey like to throw his hat in the ring? You bet he would, he said, and Bud had hired him and schooled him about what it meant to uphold the law, to be a man who could resist the chance to do wrong when it was offered, which it would be, Bud said, because of the frequency with which a lawman rubbed elbows with the criminal element. "Lie down with dogs, you get up with fleas," his mother used to say, but Bud had wanted his deputies flea proof.

"I have lost my best friend," he told the mob on the night of April 25, 1925. "But if Bud was here, he would say 'We are sworn to uphold the law,' and that's just what I intend to do. I ain't scared of heaven or hell," he said. "And I'll shoot the first man makes a move for that door."

He'd seen his share of bad situations. You couldn't kick in the doors of all the blind tiger joints he and Bud had raided or execute the liquor raids they'd gone on and not run into a couple of them. He and Bud had crept through many a thick stand of pines out in Little Hell Hole Swamp, hoping to surprise a solitary man running a steamer outfit, only to find a dozen men lounging in a clearing, each with a pistol stashed in pocket or waistband and not one of them cowed by the sound of the word *law* or the sight of the two men who'd come in its name. Bud had taught him that at those times you stated your business, then you looked sharp and waited to see which way it was going to swing. Because there was always a moment in any showdown when you felt the cord of danger twist so tight it had to snap, and when it did, the people you were facing were either going to go for their guns or throw them down and surrender.

So, on that April night he'd stood in the jailhouse door and held his shotgun in plain sight with both hammers thumbed back, while Arthur and Mack stood beside him with their shotguns at the ready too. Not that three guns would have counted for much against the firepower in that crowd. He knew that, and he'd stood his ground, and what he'd felt then was as bare and clean and true as any feeling would ever be: It wasn't just his weapon that was holding back the crowd; it was *him.* It was hard to read their faces in the wavering torchlight, but he'd wanted them to see his, so he took off his hat and stood directly under the lightbulb that hung beneath the tin awning that shaded the jailhouse door. In a crowd like that one, there was always one man who threw the switch, and you needed to find him right quick and divine which way he was going to swing, so he peered around the torchlight until his eyes lit on a horse-faced man near the front of the pack. Yes, there he was.

Finally, the man spoke. "Stand aside, Aubrey," he said, "we're taking those niggers." The voice was familiar; he came from down in Horse Creek Valley—Graniteville maybe, Langley or Clearwater. Aubrey told the man again that he was sworn to uphold the law and that he intended to do that. He saw the man hesitate; then the long face sagged, and he looked around for someone to back him up. Aubrey felt a little give in the mob, and he pushed at the spot where it had gone soft. "You men go on home now," he said. Back in the crowd other men began to shift their weight and spit on the ground, and he knew he had them. "Give us the niggers," someone called from the back, without conviction.

"You all go on home now," Aubrey Timmerman said. "Let's put an end to this long, sad day and let the law take its course."

By this time J. P. Gibson would have finished one cigarette, but Aubrey would wait while he rolled another; he had more to say. When Gibson lit up again and said, "Proceed," he'd say that the reason he'd gone on at such length and in such detail about that first night was to focus Mr. J. P. Gibson's cold amber eye and his shrewd cold mind on one question: Why would Aubrey Timmerman risk his life to save those people on one occasion and then invite the mob in to take them on another? Such an act would be evidence of a corrupted character, he would say, and he was not prepared to hand down that verdict against himself.

Had he made mistakes on the night in October? No doubt about it. He shouldn't have gone home and left Robert Bates alone at the jail, knowing that Robert sometimes lost his head in a pinch. That had been a lapse that he would answer for at God's great judgment seat. And maybe he didn't fight as hard as he could have when the men swarmed into the jail, their faces wrapped to the eyes in dark cloth. But the electric line had been cut; they'd knocked his flashlight out of his hands. They'd overpowered him and marched up the steps and ordered him to unlock the cells.

Now, he wasn't saying that those three Longs didn't deserve to die for murdering Bud. They were guilty as sin, and everybody knew it. The boys would have been long dead by now if that colored lawyer hadn't started poking holes in the first verdict until the high court sent them back down to Aiken for another trial. Had anyone thought to ask N. R. Latham what his part had been in getting three of his own people killed? Yes sir, he'd say, Aubrey Timmerman had prayed for justice, the way any other law-abiding, red-blooded, Anglo-Saxon man in any town or county in the state would have done. And yes, he was mad as hell when the judge set Dempsey Long free and made a liar of the one man—himself—who'd tried all day to keep a lid on the situation by advising the riled-up citizenry to let the law take its course. And yes, he'd sent Arthur out to pick up Dempsey Long again and serve him with the outstanding warrant for assault and battery and put him back in jail. He'd done all that, yes sir.

But it was a hell of a leap from there to what the Rainey girl said he'd done. It was a far cry from being mad as hell at a miscarriage of justice to climbing those steps, talking and laughing, to unlock Bessie Long's cell and hand her over to a mob. What kind of man would do something like that? No man like the man he knew himself to be. And he was no human buzzard either.

The sheriff opened the desk drawer again, pulled out a wooden ruler, and used it to guide the pencil down the middle of the next page of his pad of paper. In times like these a man should be able to tell friend from foe. In the left-hand column he listed the names of the men he could count on. Frank Bell, he wrote, and McLendon and Robert Bates, James Edwin Manning and Finley, the lumberman. He might be fond of the sound of his own voice, but he would stand with you. To the right of the line, in the enemy's column, he wrote John Moseley and Ella Rainey and Charlie George, the stationmaster down at Warrenville, who'd been almost as loud as Moseley in running his name into the dirt. Col. Earl Henderson, he wrote. The man who'd hustled up to the bench after the judge dismissed the charges against Dempsey Long and told him that lynching was in the air. Then he lifted the pencil. The next name he needed to decide where to put was harder to place than any other: Howard Aimar. Mr. High-and-Mighty himself, who only last week had turned from his office door when Aubrey Timmerman called out to him and looked down at the sheriff like he'd never seen him before.

Now when the sheriff closed his eyes and let the scene run, he saw himself speeding north out the Columbia Highway, passing car after car heading back toward town. But he'd driven on anyway, found the dirt track that ran along the edge of a field, and followed it until he came to a clearing in the pines. He remembered dust smoking in the headlights and a dog that barked and barked.

He remembered getting out of his car, looking up at the sliver of moon, and thinking God Almighty, somebody bring a light. The woman was on the ground with her dress on fire, and by its light and by the light of a lantern set on a pine stump he'd seen the two boys lying dead and a few men prowling the outskirts of that dim province. He will tell any jury in the land that Howard Aimar was among the prowlers. He'd drawn his pistol, said, "Stop in the name of the law." The others ran, but Howard Aimar just stood there like he'd been turned to stone while the sheriff beat at the fire in Bessie Long's clothes with his own two hands, and when it was out and he looked up again, Aimar had disappeared. But he was sure it was him; he will put his hand on the Bible and swear that the man was there that night. What troubled him was that Aimar could return the favor.

8

Howard Aimar

June 1943

CECILE KISSES HIS forehead. "Papa," she whispers, as though Papa were a saint's name, like the name he'd taken at Confirmation: Stephen, the church's first martyr.

"Get some rest, my love, you'll feel better in the morning," Libba says slowly, softly, as if she were calming a child. Her lips brush his forehead; her hand smooths his hair. Fresh air and sunshine, optimism, exercise, and rest: these are Libba's prescriptions for health and well-being. At home he likes to tease her and Cecile while they touch their toes twenty-five times in front of an open window. Sometimes Cecile flounces off, and Libba scolds him: "Can't you stop, Howard? You always go too far." He wants to promise her that when he comes home well and strong he will never tease either of his girls again; he will take everything they do and say seriously.

If they are leaving, it must be night. "Don't go," he says, but they go anyway; everybody leaves except for Lewis's daughter, the curious grandchild. When the door closes behind them, he lets out the breath it seems he's been holding all day. With Libba and Cecile gone, he does not have to be brave. He can let himself feel the sickness break his bones and burn away everything but his mind, which stays clear and full of light, like a bright room inside a dark house.

Lewis's daughter sits beside his bed, her green coat buttoned up under her chin. It must be cold where she's come from, or else she makes it cold because he feels chilled now, too, on this warm summer night. If Libba were here, she would notice his shivering and find a blanket, but Lewis's child doesn't seem to care. There's something quick and hungry about the way she watches him and waits, the way women always seem to wait for him to make something right. She's just the latest in the long line of women whom he must please. Well, he's sorry, but he does not have the strength for it any longer. "What do you want?" he says. "Why dredge up that awful time again?" he says.

Because it's part of the silence that was handed down to me, she says. *Like the old gun that went to my brother, like our mother's china came to me. I'm taking an inventory. I want to know what you left me.*

"You think I didn't regret what happened to those people?"

From the way she ducks her head and frowns, he sees that is exactly what she thinks.

"Now you listen to me," he says. Perhaps if she understood how things were for him back in 1926, she would be gentler, kinder, more forgiving; understanding and a little sympathy are all he's ever wanted, from anyone. He tells her that first and foremost, there was the pressure to make sufficient money to feed and clothe and house Libba and Lewis and Cecile. To buy laying mash for the chickens, a new Ford automobile, and everything in between. Enough money to keep them safe and sound and convince Libba's parents that their daughter had not made a disastrous marriage.

Before it could be spent, of course, money had to be earned. And unless a man's family was able to give him money, which his family was not, he had to hustle. He couldn't sit back and wait for opportunity to knock; he had to run after it, which was exactly what he'd done. Not long after the killings, he'd gone out and offered his services to a prominent member of the tribe of rich men who spent a pleasant few months in town every spring.

They'd sat in leather chairs on opposite sides of a long table in the rich man's paneled library, its shelves lined with green, maroon, and brown leather bound books, and the man had outlined what was needed. Could Howard supervise the upkeep of the big brick house and see that the polo ponies and the riding horses stood on fresh straw everyday in their long brick stable with the white cupola on top? "I can do that for you, yes sir," he said. Would he guarantee that the clay tennis court was dragged and sprinkled with water and rolled after every match? "Without fail," he said.

"Look here, Aimar," the rich man said. "How long before that business with the colored people gets straightened out?"

"Any day now, sir," he answered. "I'm sure of it." He poured the rich man a small glass of spirits. "My own private reserve," he said, and the rich man had rolled the whiskey in his mouth, swallowed and smiled and held out his hand.

To make money, you had to hustle, and you had to make a place for yourself that no one else could occupy. That was why, when the president of the Lions Club asked him to offer the toast at their annual banquet, he said consider it done. And when an officer of the Rotary Club invited him to chair a committee, he never turned him down.

"If I had a coat of arms," he says, "the motto would be 'Happy to Oblige.'" In return his friends in the Rotary Club and the Knights of Columbus, the Lions Club and the Chamber of Commerce, thought highly of him; they wished him well then, and they wish him well now; they will always wish him well. In a crunch they will stand shoulder to shoulder; they will vouch for one another.

That was why when Frank Henderson called at five-thirty one morning in early November of 1926 and said, "We need you to get down to the depot, Howard," he'd gotten up and hustled down there. An hour earlier Frank's uncle in Columbia had called to say that two bundles of the *World* had just been loaded onto the southbound train. You couldn't miss Barrett's stories, he said—top of the front page of both editions, under the biggest headlines: "Sheriff Is Accused of Complicity with the Lynchers of Three" and "S.C. Whispers Names of Mob Killers."

"Of course I went," he says. Has she not been listening? Did he have a choice? He picked up the papers then walked over to his office and read the stories. The story about the sheriff held no surprises, though the word *complicity* troubled him, so he pulled out his *Webster's* and looked it up. Then it troubled him more. People had been accusing each other of complicity since 1656, and in all that time the meaning had not changed. *Association or participation in or as if in a wrongful act.* Any direction you tried to run, that definition would stop you. Between the *association* and the *as if,* there was no way out.

"Up and down Horse Creek Valley," the whispering story began, "men have talked of murder for a month. In small frame houses, squatting between cotton fields and the twisting red clay roads, in offices and in stores, the names of the lynchers have been whispered behind locked doors."

But none of the men he knew had whispered the names of any lynchers; they didn't know any lynchers, only each other, and themselves.

No sooner had he finished the papers and opened the office at nine than the bell on the back of the front door rang and Aubrey Timmerman himself came in. "Speak of the devil," Howard said, but the sheriff didn't find that funny. His clothes looked slept in, his face was red, and he was squinting like a man who'd just finished working a long shift under bright lights. He had the palest blue eyes, with a light in them that reminded Howard of the look of the sky in the hottest part of the summer, and when someone else talked, the sheriff seemed to watch him from a place way back inside his skull.

"I didn't like a single thing about the man," Howard says. "Not his hands with their new pink skin nor his gun belt that creaked when he shifted in his chair." Above all, he disliked the sheriff's voice. It was distinctive and strident, like a blue jay's call. "What can I do for you, sheriff?" Howard said, and Aubrey Timmerman leaned across the desk and lowered his voice. He was making the rounds, he said, carrying the same message to friend and foe: He intended to charge with perjury any man who said that Aubrey Timmerman was at the scene when the Longs were killed. He'd put him on the stand, make him swear on the Bible and tell *his* part. And the whole time the sheriff talked, the word *complicity* coursed through Howard's mind. "You pass the word along, I'd be obliged," the sheriff said.

"Will do," Howard said, and then he slapped the desk with both palms, to show that the conversation was over.

"Now I was not without sympathy for the man," he says to the curious grandchild; she needs to hear that part of the story too. Everyone in town knew how hard Barrett had been dogging the sheriff. No man could stand up to the pressure to remember what the sheriff was being challenged to recall. They all knew how murky things could get when what *really* happened got so tangled up with what *should* have happened, it was hard to tell them apart, especially when a man mistook what he'd *meant* to do for what he'd *actually* done. He knew how difficult it was to examine your conscience, to work your way through the commandments on the lookout for the smallest sin. *Have I broken any private vow? Have I cursed anyone or otherwise wished evil on him? Have I cooperated in the sins of others?* There are as many sins as there are days in a week, hours in a day, actions of the hand, movements of the eye, intentions of the heart. And the lack or failure or withholding of those same actions and movements and intentions are also sins. "What have I failed to do?" he says. "No one ever gets to the bottom of that question, and that is the truth."

But she doesn't feel the least bit sorry for him. She's getting restless: looking at him mournfully, reproachfully, like every other woman he's disappointed. He must gather up the last remaining scraps of his strength and tell her something that will keep her from leaving and taking his life with her. "Put yourself in my place," he says. She looks startled by the invitation, as though no one had ever asked that of her. "We all knew that Albert Long killed Sheriff Glover. It's hard to imagine that a boy of fourteen could heft a shotgun, much less fire one with deadly aim, but he did. Because his own people said he did, that's how I know."

"The woman, Bessie Long, his own flesh and blood, accused him, and Dr. Hastings wrote it down on his prescription pad." He has her attention now; she looks bright and rapacious again. *I've seen it,* she says. *One page that ends in the middle of a sentence.* Now she's greedy to hear the rest.

"I will try," he says. "I will do my best. This is all I have ever tried to do, so help me God." Dr. Hastings was called to the Long house on that April day, and there he found Sheriff Earl Glover and Mamie Long lying dead; he found Bessie Long shot in the arm and chest and gut. "Shot all to pieces" was the way he always put it, dying. But he had some men load her into the backseat of his car anyway; he climbed in with her, and another man drove them to the Negro infirmary at Leesville.

As they jolted along the road, she groaned and wept and called on Jesus and spilled her blood. She was sometimes awake and sometimes so far gone that he had to hold his hand under her nose and feel her breath to know she was alive. During one period of quiet and clarity he told her that he did not think she could be saved. And if she was going to die, he said, didn't she want to meet her maker with a clear conscience? Didn't she want to tell him which one of her kin had fired the rounds of No. 6 shot that had ripped through the sheriff's lungs and heart?

"Yes," she whispered. "Albert."

"What's that you say? Your brother?"

"Cousin."

"But when they got to Leesville, Bessie Long was still alive," he says. "And your great-grandfather removed the bullets and stitched up her wounds. He patched her up, and she stood trial with the rest of her family. And being recommended to the mercy of the court, she was sentenced to prison for the rest of the life he'd given back to her."

He's told the story as clearly and simply as he can manage, leaving nothing out, trying to show her how it was, and he thinks he's succeeded.

My great-grandfather, she says, and then she sits quietly, head bowed, studying her hands. But soon she's restless again. Twice she shakes her head, stands up, pulls her coat tightly around her, takes a few steps toward the door.

"What do you want from me?" he says.

Your story, she says. *Tell me what you did that you called unforgivable.*

"Sit down," he says, but she will not. She opens the door, looks up and down the hall. She's going; just the idea of it makes him feel weak, weaker than he's been, as though when she walks away from him she carries off his strength. "Wait," he says. "Stop. Don't go."

The night the Longs were killed, he went to his office, and he meant to stay there. He had enough work to keep him there all night. Policies to be written; the height of a column of red numbers in the ledger measured against a second column of black figures, to see which one was winning that month. There were envelopes to be opened and letters read that he'd put off reading for too long. A contract to be drawn up for the rich man to sign, summing up their recent understanding. But the longer he sat there and thought of what Bessie Long had said about Albert and remembered N. R. Latham's contempt for the lawful verdict and sentence the court had handed down, and when he thought of the men who would be expecting him to be there to see the wrong of Earl Glover's death righted, he knew he could not stay.

He joined the line of automobiles moving up the Columbia Highway. Then, just outside the city limits, he began to think of Albert Long. He remembered the scrawny neck and bony shoulders that he'd stared at throughout the three days of the trial. He remembered how Albert Long had squirmed in his seat, how he'd fidgeted and knocked his knees together the way Lewis did when he got restless. And once his thinking started to run in that direction, he couldn't stop it, and before long, all he could think about was that Albert Long was not much older than Lewis. And that's when he stumbled on the real reason he was driving out the Columbia Highway. At school, at church, at home, he'd been taught that the force of one man's character was sufficient unto any evil day, and with every mile he drove he was more convinced of what he would do when he got there.

He would push to the front of the crowd, step out in front of all those guns. He'd grab a torch, haul Albert into the light. "Stop," he'd say, and they would stop. "He's just a boy," he'd say, and the other men would wake up and see that he was right. He would tell them that for the sake of their neighbors and the town they loved, for the sake of their own immortal souls, they must not descend into savagery and lawlessness. They must not descend.

But when he got to where everybody was going, it was pitch-black dark. "It was so dark you could not make out the face of the man standing next to you," he says. They were in a clearing with a black wall of pines all around, a black sky overhead, the hard ridges of old plowed ground underfoot. There was a big crowd, a lot of confusion. "Human buzzards," Wesley Barton called the men who were there that night.

There might have been some of that breed there, he doesn't know. What he knows is that he went there to stop it. He tried. "It does not matter how I tried," he says, "because I got there too late. They were dead," he says. "Do you hear me? All three of them, dead." That was what was unforgivable, he tells her: that he got there too late to stop the other men from doing what they did.

When he's done, he sees that she is sitting beside his bed again, but it doesn't matter. Telling that story has taken his strength, and what has left him will not return. "You've gotten what you came for," he says. "Now stay or go, but let me rest."

9

Libba Aimar

November 1926

SHE AND HER mother called the letters they wrote one another their *good talks*. Before her mother forgave her for eloping with Howard, she and Libba had exchanged brief notes at the end of every week. Once her parents had accepted that Libba was a married woman living with her husband in her own house, the habit of writing to one another was so pleasurable for both of them that they kept it up. When she or her mother traveled, longer letters crossed the distance between them. Even now, some mornings when the house was quiet, she would close the bedroom door and sit at the small maple desk near the window that looked out into a magnolia tree and write her mother a letter. When she was done, she would put it in a hatbox on the top shelf of her closet where no one would have any business looking until she was gone, and what would it matter then?

"Dearest Mother," she wrote. "Or maybe *Madame Chairman* would be more fitting, since it is to you that I still imagine submitting the minutes of my life. At this time of the year, with the flower show upon us, I feel your presence more than ever. I have a lot to live up to, Mother, and don't I know it? Your spirit shares a hymnal with me every Sunday and sits beside me at the dinner table, ever the exemplar of courtesy, tact, gentle grace, subtle mental force, unselfishness and kindness, patience and love, the full range of virtues that marked you as the great lady you were and *are* and always will be. Now, this year, if the truth be known, Mother, you have begun to dim in my memory, because the living can only follow the dead for so long, and then we must turn back. Still, if I forget who you were and are, the pictures in my hallway remind me. There you are, in a smart hat and gloves, gavel raised, presiding over the statewide meeting of the Federation of Women's Clubs. Standing tall, you address the Daughters of the American Revolution, the United Daughters of the Confederacy. A dozen times a day, especially when I am perplexed or troubled, the proverbs you dispensed so freely come back to me. *There is a salve for every sore,* I'll think. *Sufficient unto the day is the evil thereof.*

"If I forget you, others remember for me. Every Christmas Eve after midnight Mass, where I have once again ascended the musical heights and hit the high C in "O Holy Night," a woman will take me aside and squeeze my hands, kiss my cheek. 'When I closed my eyes,' she will say, 'I could almost believe your mother was in the choir loft again.'

"Every year, so I'm told, the Civic Club Christmas baskets for the poor look more like the ones you filled and delivered all over the county. 'Our Lady Bountiful,' the newspaper called you, and in the picture printed above that caption you looked the part: you in your fur-trimmed cloak, the baskets arrayed at your feet, my brother Lewis and I standing on either side of you, abiding under the shelter of your wings.

"I write to you now because I do not know what to do or think or where to turn for advice about what is going on here in town, but you always knew, or you *acted* like you did, which is, as you taught me, practically the whole task life requires of us. Even on the day when the telegram came, you wouldn't open it or let anyone else open it either. The war was over, you said. Your son could not be dead. But that sniper in France hadn't heard the news.

"Howard recommends that I limit my newspaper reading to the social pages and my progress reports on the flower show. No doubt you would second his opinion. 'Don't read the papers if it bothers you so much,' I hear you say. 'Never trouble trouble till trouble troubles you.' But I do read them, and even if I didn't, I can't go down to Hahn's or to the Savoy for a Coca-Cola, to church or a club meeting, without somebody showing me a clipping or quoting what's being said about us in a newspaper somewhere in the state or in the articles that New York reporter writes about us.

"Ladies, ladies, I tell the Little Garden Club, after all our dear town has endured, doesn't everyone deserve some cheering up? Let's work to make this the best flower show ever, I say. Beyond this glass, through which we see but darkly, lies the untroubled vastness of God's design, in which all is destined and ordained. In due time the guilty will be caught and punished. And shame on anyone who has suggested that the blight has spread beyond a few depraved individuals to everyone. Still, the damage has been done. You cannot forget what you know. I know that Wesley Barton called our men human buzzards at a feast, and I know that the woman crawled among the crowd that night, begging them not to kill her, and I can't erase either picture from my mind. What would it be like, I ask myself, to crawl and plead for your life and find no help or mercy? To search every face and see no kindness?

"The morning after it happened, I saw Papa and Howard talking in the yard. Papa banged his cane on the ground the way he does when he demands to be heard, and Howard paced and pressed both hands to the top of his head as though trying to keep the thoughts from flying out. I raised the kitchen window and stood at the sink, washing a coffee cup and listening. 'Yes, Howard,' Papa said. 'Sometimes it takes a violent storm to clear the air.' Whenever Howard repeats those words to me, I imagine a summer storm: smothering air and black clouds and sudden wind that rips leaves from the trees and a hard rain beating on the ground. Then the sky clears as abruptly as it darkened, the clouds gallop off to the east. But if what Howard says is true, and the violent storm has passed, where is the brighter day that follows? Why is the air still as thick and murky and black as the plague of darkness that God once called down on Egypt? A darkness to be felt, is how the Bible describes it, a darkness in which they did not see one another. That is what it is like here now.

"I am glad you are not still in this world to see what it has come to, Mother. Two days ago, in the ballroom of the Highland Park Hotel, Zeke was up on the ladder, cleaning the windows, as he does every year before the flower show, and in passing I said, 'Remember, Zeke, no soap on those windows. Use muslin and clean water. Remember to add some lemon juice to soften the water, and use a cotton cloth dipped in a little alcohol to add brilliancy . . .' But in the middle of my instructions, he interrupted me—and he didn't even bother to turn around on the ladder when he spoke—just kept wiping the windows, with that infernal hat shoved forward at its usual cocky angle. "I know how to do your job, Miz Libba," he said. "Been doing it since I could climb a ladder."

"I will tell you something else, Mother, knowing you cannot hear me. The darkness has even come between Howard and me. You always taught me that a wife should be a helpmate to her husband, and I've tried. *Her lamp does not go out at night,* I tell myself when I wake in the middle of the night and see Howard's empty bed and know he's downstairs, worrying. I say it again as I go down and find him sitting at the little kitchen table in his blue flannel robe, staring at nothing. And I say it once again as I stand behind his chair and stroke his hair back from his forehead until, slowly, as though he were giving in to temptation, he lets his head relax against me.

"Your words are a lamp unto my feet in all times and circumstances, except one. You spoke only once of what you called 'the married embrace' as something to be welcomed, or at least accepted, as an inevitable circumstance of the matrimonial state. But you would shudder at the thought of the embraces to which I am subjected. Every night since those people were killed, Howard comes to my bed or pulls me into his, and what he wants, I can never seem to give him. 'Lie still, Libba,' he says one night, and the next night I am not lively enough, and no matter how diligently I search for them, no words come to explain this to me, and I feel I have become the voice of one crying in the wilderness of her own bedroom.

"Yesterday, as on every Sunday morning, I got Lewis dressed and fed and ready to go to the nine o'clock Mass with Howard. Lewis looked so handsome in his gray sweater vest, his clean white shirt and gray slacks, with silky hair neatly parted and combed to one side. "Such a little gentleman," I said, and I knelt to straighten his tie.

"He put a hand on my shoulder, looked into my eyes, and said, 'Come with us, Mother.' He looked so serious and hopeful, as though his heart might break if I said no. And I knew instantly what section of the *Baltimore Catechism* he'd been studying. I could have marched up to his room and picked up that book from his nightstand and opened it to the exact page.

Q: Are all bound to belong to the church?
A: All are bound to belong to the church, and he who knows the church to be the true church and remains out of it cannot be saved.

"That page is marked with one of the cards the nuns hand out to the children at St. Angela's as rewards for good conduct and memorization. On the front of this card is a picture of Jesus, Mary, and Joseph, with *The Holy Family* in gold script underneath, and on the back are the words 'Jesus, Mary and Joseph, pray for us. 100 days indulgence.' I asked him once what that business of the hundred days meant, and he explained that every time a Catholic said that phrase, one hundred days were subtracted from the time certain people had to spend in purgatory. 'What kind of people?' I asked. Unbaptized babies and the misguided or ignorant others who'd died outside the Roman Catholic Church, he said. 'The Poor Souls,' he called them.

"And I knew it would do no good to explain to my son that because I neither knew nor accepted that the Catholic Church was the one true church, I could not be lost or condemned. That reasoning would be beyond him. But I ask myself: What kind of people torment a child with visions of his own mother shivering outside the gates of paradise, waiting for enough Catholics to whisper 'Jesus, Mary, and Joseph' so she can go in?

"But rather than make an issue of it, I said, 'Thank you for the sweet invitation, Lewis Hastings. But I have my own church. Now go outside, please, and wait for your father, and don't you get down on the ground in those good clothes.' Poor soul or no, I am still his mother, and when he examines his conscience every week before making his little confession, he has to ask himself if he's disobeyed me. His little catechism says so.

"But that all happened yesterday, Mother, and today is today, another one of your lessons, expressed so aptly in lines by our favorite South Carolina poetess, Elizabeth Reese, where grief departs and joy comes in: 'And every lad his love can win / For here is April weather.' Granted, it is November now, not April, but the sentiment holds true no matter the season. I woke up early this morning, full of energy. It was barely light outside when Minnie arrived to help me with the household inventory. You are the one who taught me the pleasures of our twin yearly chores: the fall inventory and the spring cleaning. Two poles of the axis on which our domestic globe spins. It was you who taught me so long and so well that there are certain things that no home should lack, others that cannot be tolerated. Without surrounding ourselves with quality and beauty that heals and rests the soul, you said, how shall we live? You are the one who instructed me in the vigilance we must maintain to guard against the rot and wear that can so quickly drag our lives down into the shabby depths.

"Thanks to you, I know that egg white applied with a small camel's hair paintbrush and rubbed gently with a soft cloth will remove flyspecks from gilt frames. I know that cut glass must be washed in hot soapsuds and not dried but left to drain; that silver is to be washed in a basin by itself and never touched with a greasy cloth. And my knowledge of household minutiae is matched and amplified by Minnie's of washing and ironing.

"If I close my eyes, I can see her and Zeke now, the two of them walking down the driveway, each carrying a suitcase. She wore a plain yellow dress, and her hair was done up in two neat braids pinned across the top of her head. She was tall and skinny as a crane and carried herself with great dignity, as she still does. For the first week they lived here, Zeke ran and hid his face in her skirt whenever Howard or I spoke to him, until one day I took his hand. 'You are too big to hide in your mother's skirt,' I said. 'Everybody must earn his keep here, Zeke.' And I led him toward the house. Minnie walked along behind us for a little way, saying, 'Go on now, son. Nobody's going to hurt you,' and I put him to work sorting kindling on the back porch and gave him a glass of buttermilk when he was done, and after that we were square.

"But I could never tell Minnie any of this now. I am reluctant to reminisce with her about pleasant memories of our time together because she no longer seems to share them. Like how good it used to be to come down the stairs amid the aroma of coffee and bacon and hear Howard and Minnie joking and laughing in the kitchen.

"'Minnie,' he would say. 'Did you and that rooster work out your differences this morning?'

"And she would laugh and say, 'Go on, now, Mr. Howard, that rooster knows better than to mess with me.'

"Then Howard would say had he ever told her she made the best grits in the world, and what was her secret? Just put them in the pot with water and salt and a little pat of butter, she'd say, and back and forth like that they would go.

"These days she just plunks down Howard's plate of poached eggs and grits and bacon cooked the way he likes them: the yokes dry and crumbly, the bacon crisp, the grits served with a little pat of melted butter in the middle. He hardly bothers to look up when he says, 'Thank you,' and the dining room door has already swung shut behind her before I hear, or imagine, her saying, 'You're welcome, Mr. Howard.' Only now, more often than not, she'll catch herself and say Mr. Aimar. Mr. Aimar, Mrs. Aimar, that's who we are to her now, no matter how often I correct her. 'Minnie, I am put out with you,' I say. 'How many times have I asked you to call me Miz Libba?'

"'Yes, ma'am, Miz Libba,' she says. 'Looks like it just slips my mind sometimes.' But the next time it's right back to Mrs. Aimar again, and it has begun to seem like a deliberate act of defiance that Minnie, who can go down to Hahn's with a grocery list in her head and money in her pocket and come back with every item bought and every penny accounted for, can't remember from one hour to the next what the woman who pays and houses and feeds her wants to be called. And then I remember your calm forbearance in the face of provocation, and I calm myself with your wisdom. *Least said, soonest mended.*

"I even bought two tickets from Minnie to the upcoming performance at Schofield School by the violinist Joseph Douglass, an event I read about in the paper to which black *and* white are cordially invited. Joseph Douglass, so Minnie told me, is the grandson of Frederick Douglass, but when I said, 'I don't believe I know that name, Minnie,' she winced like a sudden pain had pierced her. The tickets are being sold, Minnie says, to send a deserving child to the school, and I am happy to support that cause, even though Papa swears that the money from ticket sales is going straight into the pockets of the colored lawyer from Columbia who's helping Herbert Long secure the two thousand dollars for each of his family dead that he feels entitled to by state law. Six thousand dollars is more money than many honest white men make in a year of hard work, Papa says. So what are the chances of that much money going to the colored father of murderers?

"I've come to expect Howard's morning gloominess, the way he pokes at his eggs, mashes grits with the back of the fork and complains that they're cold. But he looked especially glum when I told him that today was household inventory day. Then, once I'd gotten him a little cheered up and blown him a dozen kisses from the back steps and boosted Lewis onto Zeke's wagon and sent him off to school, I went inside and poured myself a cup of coffee from the blue-speckled percolator on the stove. 'Minnie, get yourself a cup,' I said. 'Come sit down with me for a minute.'

"We went into the dining room, but I was the only one carrying a cup. Minnie sat on the edge of her chair, flicking her dustrag at her shoes. 'Minnie,' I said. 'I wish you'd tell me what we're going to do about that child's bed-wetting.' Lewis's sheets had been sopping again this morning, and we've puzzled that problem through together more times than I can count. Minnie has always been as full of advice and sympathy as if Lewis were her own child. But no sooner had the question left my mouth this morning than she said, 'I surely don't know, Mrs. Aimar,' and she went back to flicking at her shoes. 'Zeke never gave me any trouble that way,' she said. 'I best be getting back to work.' And she did just that, and I sat there staring into my coffee, feeling my whole face get hot.

"I was so flustered that I had to go to the front room and stand at the window and think. Here I was, chasing after Minnie, practically begging her to let things go back to the way they've always been, wishing I could tell her plainly that what happened to those three colored people was a shame, an abomination, a disgrace. But you can't blame the entire white race for the actions of its lawless elements. Of course, I would say to her, the guilty should be punished, but what does that have to do with us? Howard was working at his office when those people were killed. How could he know, as that northern reporter claims we *all* know, who was there? You can't believe everything you see or hear; you can't go around repeating slander.

"We worked together all morning. We know our jobs so well we could do them in our sleep. In the butler's pantry Minnie pulled napkins and tablecloths from the drawers, unfolded each one and held it up to the light so I could inspect it for signs of wear or stains too firmly set into the weave to be expunged. She folded the items that had passed inspection and put the others in a box then handed me the juice glasses one by one, and I looked for chips or cracks or wear in the gilt rims.

"At noon I splashed my face and neck with cool water from the kitchen tap. I went upstairs and changed into a presentable dress and fixed my hair and went back down to eat dinner with Howard. Lady peas and rice and a pork chop, tea with sprigs of fresh mint from the clump that grows rampant in the sunny spot under the outside faucet. While we ate, I read to him from the list I'd been keeping: so many tea towels and napkins discarded; so many threadbare sheets ripped up for rags.

"While I read, he looked like he was trying to swallow a rock, so I patted his arm to show him that it would be all right. I sit on his lap sometimes and tease him about being an old miser, but in fact he is a generous man. One year, at the close of household inventory day, when he thought I'd gone upstairs to bed, I tiptoed into the kitchen and saw him on the back porch, taking napkins out of the box I'd left there for Minnie to dispose of and holding each one up to the light. I know him so well, I could hear him think: *Now what is wrong with that one? Has no one ever taught my sweet wife how to turn a blanket binding or patch the elbow of a sweater?*

"After Howard had his nap and went back to the office at three, we went upstairs to finish our work. I opened the chest in the upstairs hall, and there were my Lewis's baby blankets and the long white gown in which four generations of Aimars had been christened. And, oh, I don't know why, but when I unfolded the gown and shook it out and pressed it to my face, I imagined that Lewis's baby smell was still in that cloth, and such a feeling rose up in me then—longing and love and sadness, all mixed together. I said, 'Oh, Minnie, they grow up so fast.' She said, 'That is the truth, Miz Libba. Before you know it, they're running for their own train, and you still trying to hand them their lunch pail.' And for a fleeting moment it was just like old times again. And then I glanced out of the hall window that looks out onto one of Howard's pecan trees. A noisy flock of crows were cawing and squabbling there, and Wesley Barton's buzzards came flapping into my head, and I handed Minnie the gown and walked down there and yanked the shade down to the sill.

"I know that you remember old Miss Mattie Weeks. Every Christmas season when I was a child, you'd fix her a basket of oranges and fruitcake and divinity and pecans. Papa would drive us in the buggy to her house, and I would run up the front walk between the ragged box-wood hedges and set it on the porch. Two weeks or a month later the basket would still be there, faded ribbon flapping in the breeze. We always wondered what in the world would make a person shut herself up that way, but today, when I pulled down the blind, I felt in myself how a person might come to believe that closing the world out was the only way to make it go on being what you wanted it to be and believed it was.

"When I couldn't put it off any longer, we went down to the hall closet. I pulled the string; the light came on. We worked our way through the winter coats and down the line of shoes, and then I had to ask. Minnie would have thought it strange if I hadn't. 'Minnie,' I said, 'do you know what became of Mr. Aimar's shoes that I left here?'

"'I threw them out, Mrs. Aimar,' she said, running her rag around the doorknob. 'You said they were ruined, so I took care of them. I thought that's what you'd want me to do.'

"'Well, that's that,' I said. 'If Mr. Aimar asks after them, you send him to me.' *All wrong will end,* I heard you say, and I felt like a flock of birds had taken off inside me and flown up into the sun."

10

Minnie Settles

November 1926

LIKE MOST LIES, the one she'd told Libba was a mix of truth and silence. It was true that she'd taken care of the shoes. What she hadn't said was that Zeke had found the croker sack on her back porch, and after she'd told him what she knew, the sack had disappeared. Now she was worried sick. What was also unsaid was how dismayed she'd felt to see the relief on Libba's face when she'd learned that the shoes were gone.

By the end of any other household inventory she would have collected her own pile of cast-off hats and coats, blouses and trousers, blankets and napkins and glasses. In another year she would have kept some things for herself and some for Zeke, set aside others for the annual rummage sale at Mt. Hebron Baptist Church or to be given to the down-and-out, the helpless, the shiftless. But this year, for the first time since she'd come to work for them, she'd taken no castoffs from their house. All stains were suspect now; this year she was taking nothing home but two plates of the chicken and rice and lima beans she'd cooked for their supper and the dollar bill that Mr. Aimar had slipped into her hand in the kitchen that morning.

"Minnie," he'd said in the same confiding whisper with which he asked for her help on every household inventory day, "if you can keep my sweet wife from spending us into the poorhouse, I will be forever in your debt." She'd taken the bill—there had been no way to refuse—and slipped it into the pocket of her skirt. But she wouldn't be his ally, and so all day, whenever Libba had asked, she'd voted no. No to any napkin with the faintest stain, to a juice glass with the slightest wear on the gilt rim. No to Little Mister's winter coat with the snot-stiffened sleeves and pockets that sagged from the sticks and rocks and string he stuffed into them. Let Mr. Aimar go broke, replacing every stained and shabby thing.

She buttoned her sweater and felt Libba watching her. *What has gotten into our Minnie?* she could almost hear her thinking. She imagined herself turning on Libba, telling the truth: The killings, what else? Then she would press on. You go along and you go along, she would say, while one day folds into the next, believing that you know the white people you work for as well as you know the contents of every drawer and cabinet in their house. You know other things too, of course; you aren't deaf, dumb, and blind; you aren't simple-minded. You know that Zeke's father fled after he shot off his mouth to a deputy sheriff and the Klan came to call. You've heard about the rich colored farmer from Abbeville, Anthony Crawford, who traded testy words with a white clerk over the price of cotton one morning back in 1916 and by the next night was hanging, mutilated, from a tree out near the county fairgrounds. All your life you've heard the old people's stories about worse times and places.

Those things had happened, and you knew they'd happened, but you'd lulled yourself into believing that they happened in another world, where a lower class of white people lived than the ones you thought of as your white people. But then the Longs were killed, and Mr. Aimar came home early and tried to clean his shoes, and ever since the night when you saw him trying to wash off what would not go away, you couldn't crawl out from under the feeling that you lived in that other world now, among the people you'd only seen from a distance, and you knew what a fool you'd been to tell yourself you'd ever lived anywhere but there. And all you were trying to do now was to live like you knew where you were. Right now that meant walking down the back steps with a plate of warm food in each hand and pretending not to see Libba waving a sad little toodle-oo from the kitchen window.

Outside the air was close and still. Zeke's horse and wagon were tied to a post in front of her house. She saw light behind the front window shade, and she walked toward it, telling herself that tomorrow might be the day she'd march into the Aimar's house and quit. Every evening now, walking from their house to her own, she occupied herself with these plans. She imagined how she'd pack all her things in the one suitcase she'd brought with her. How she'd leave behind every blouse Libba had ever given her, every faded, curled photograph of Zeke and Lewis, of herself with Lewis and Cecile at the beach. She'd take special pleasure in abandoning the wren's nest that had strands of her hair woven in among the twigs and fluff. Libba had picked it up in the yard one day and given it to her: proof, she'd said, of how firmly Minnie was woven into their family.

Every night she packed her possessions, left everything they'd given her, climbed up into Zeke's wagon. But that was as far as she ever got. She couldn't imagine where he'd take her or what she would do next. Schofield School would keep her name on the list of graduates that people consulted when they wanted to hire some help, but once word got around that she'd walked out on a family like the Aimars, it would be hard to find work with another that would give her a house and meals and two dollars a week and pay to have her teeth worked on or fix it with the sheriff if Zeke got liquored up on a Saturday night and got thrown in jail.

Then she was home, and Zeke was there, as familiar a part of the one big room where she lived as the whitewashed fireplace, the iron bedstead, chifforobe and rocking chair, the table under the window that looked out over the washpots and the garden. He'd lit the kerosene lamp on the table, laid out knives and forks. He'd brought in water from the cistern and tidied himself up, the way he knew she liked for him to do before supper: washed his hands and face, brushed off his overalls, and buttoned his blue shirt all the way up under his chin. "It's fixing to storm," she said, handing him the plates. She closed the door, pulled the padlock through the new hasp he'd mounted there, chased the thought of quitting from her mind.

"Sit down, Mama," he said. "Take a load off." Sitting across from her at the table in the lantern light, he looked like his father.

He was talking when the downpour started; it made such a racket

95

on the tin roof that she wasn't sure she'd heard him right. The lantern flame fluttered at eye level, and she ducked and dodged, trying to see around it. "Come again?" she said, and when he did, she shoved back her chair and came around the table at him, one fist cocked, the fork gripped in her other hand.

He stood to meet her and looked back and forth from the fork to her fist, as though trying to gauge which one to fear. "Whoa, Mama, easy," he said, and he grinned at her like it was funny that she was coming to knock him down, the way she'd done once or twice, just to give him a taste of what the world had in store for an ignorant colored boy with a big mouth. But his grin waxed and waned now, the way it did when he got flustered.

"You did *what?*" she said, but she'd heard him right. "How much did that man pay you?" she asked. Her heart surged up her throat. She unclenched her fist, and the fork clattered onto her plate.

The sound made Zeke startle. "He gave me his word," he said, and he wiped his whole face with one big hand.

"Better spend it while you still can," she said. She had to sit down then; she braced her hands on her knees. Her heart still pounded, but now her blood felt sluggish and thick in her veins, and she was short of breath, as if she were running up the endless flight of marble steps that sometimes appeared in her dreams. He put a hand on her shoulder, but she shrugged it off. "You're boasting, aren't you?" she said. "Proud of yourself. I hear Albert Long liked to boast a bit himself." Now Zeke wasn't smiling anymore. "I wish to God I'd dragged you with me to Jackson's and made you take a good long look at the pine needles and dirt and broken teeth and bone stuck in the mess of dried blood on what was left of that boy's face."

His face went slack, ashy. "Mama," he said. Then, feebly: "He gave me his word."

"Shit," she said. "You always were a prideful, stupid boy." Trusting too, she didn't say. Way too trusting. Her fault, for raising him that way. But how do you school your child in mistrust without mangling his whole character? She pushed through the screen door and sat in her chair on the back porch and watched the rain pour off the roof and into the barrel. She should have known better than to leave those shoes where Zeke could find them. He was always poking around in her business, looking for something he could use or sell and bring her a share of the profits. But where could she have hidden them in her house? Under the bed, to trouble her sleep? Next to her black church shoes on the floor of the chifforobe?

Why hadn't she burned them or dropped them in a pond or made them vanish in some other way? Was it because the sight of the croker sack and the weight of the shoes were proof that those killings were real? Without some tangible reminder, what had happened might settle into what the Aiken paper kept trying to make it: the scene of an inhuman horror, a crime committed by phantoms. A bucket of dirty wash water poured onto this hungry, sandy ground that soaked it up so quickly you couldn't say it had ever been anything but dry, clean sand. So she'd kept the shoes, and now look.

She sat and listened to the rain until her heart slowed. When she went back inside, Zeke was sitting at the table with his hands folded between his knees, looking sick and miserable. Well, he *should* be sick. She sat down across from him, picked up her fork. "Eat," she said. "Don't let this food go to waste." He did what he was told, one hand over his eyes. She looked at the top of his head, at the two small spirals of hair on the crown. It was the first thing she'd noticed when the midwife had handed him to her. A double swirl, for good luck, the woman had said. Maybe that luck would hold now.

She put her hand into the pocket of her skirt, found Mr. Aimar's money. He'd be forever in her debt, he'd said when he gave it to her. But that wouldn't matter once Curtis N. R. Barrett wrote about what Zeke had showed him. Howard Aimar's debt to her would be forfeit then. She took the dollar out of her pocket, slid it across the table. Zeke tried to push it back, but she said, "Take it, son. Go on. Spend it like there's no tomorrow. Don't bring me any change."

11

Curtis N. R. Barrett

November 1926

AMONG THE MIDDAY dinner crowd at the Hotel Aiken, he stood out like an unwelcome guest at a family gathering. In contrast to the businessmen dressed in flannel trousers and shirts with rolled-up sleeves or the farmers in khaki work clothes and boots, he wore a suit to meals, a crisp white shirt and tie, cuff links, signet ring, and polished shoes. Whenever he entered the dining room, conversation stopped, silverware slowed; ill will flowed toward him from every corner. Not that he minded the notoriety; he welcomed it, *invited* it. Today, as usual, he paused in the doorway then claimed the table at the front window where he sat at every meal, hoping that the sight of him might provoke a passerby into rushing inside and saying something reckless. He propped the *Aiken Standard* against the sugar bowl and ordered the dinner special: a pan-fried pork chop, bone-in, girdled with pearly fat and topped with a thin slice of onion. In his time in South Carolina he'd developed a taste for warm pig fat; he relished the last strands of pork, gnawed, nibbled, and sucked from the bone.

He did not know about the letter that had just arrived at the governor's office or how, after reading it, Arthur McCormick had walked around for ten minutes, belching quietly into one of the large white handkerchiefs his wife tucked into his pocket every morning. The letter was typed on stationery from the Hotel Courtland in Canton, Ohio, but its author was clearly a South Carolina man.

Dear Governor McCormick,

If I was governor of South Carolina, I would plant my official shoe with such vehemence on the posterior of a certain Mr. Barrett, the charlatan would taste shoe leather for a week. Not that the New York World gives a tinker's dam for law and order; if so, they would look to that quagmire of filth and licentiousness, robbery, blood, and murder, where they were spawned. But in their contempt for the South, and especially South Carolina, they will send their sewer rat reporter to Aiken to attempt to convince others that our homeland is the very seat of corruption and lawlessness. At dinner the other night a prominent judge said to me, "Well, the New York World boys are going after you people of South Carolina."

"Yes," I replied. "And we feel like a dove that a buzzard has puked on."

If I was to fully vent my feelings, the newspapers would have to publish a fireproof edition, but I do feel that I ought at least to sketch a faint adumbration of my conception of that blatherskite representative of a slanderous rag. If the devil were Barrett's daddy, old Jezebel his mother, he would disgrace both sire and dame.

As God is my witness, I would rather be a one-eyed yellow cur dog and belong to a sorry negro than give succor to this black-hearted hypocrite.

Respectfully yours,
   Haywood R. Brodie

Barrett would have found the letter rich. He loved a good fight, a story he could run with, one that might get Swope's attention by giving the editor what he called the human element—pathos and tragic irony, the stuff of life. Barrett's version might have sketched a small-bore salesman attacking his typewriter in an alcoholic rage in a grim little room in Canton then gone on to probe Haywood Brodie's motives and expose his illusions. Barrett had shed his own self-serving fantasies in

France and felt it was his right and duty to help others shed their own. "When she comes forward this week to tell the story of her friendship with Baring," he wrote in a story about a young woman betrayed by a married man, "she will be gathering for the last time the tattered ends of a childish illusion. The man she believed to be a charming, honorable friend—apparently the only friendship with a man in all her young life—she may face with manacles on his hands charged as a wife poisoner. Whether he is acquitted of that charge or not, he is already convicted of killing a child's dreams."

But he didn't know about Haywood Brodie's letter. What he *did* know was that all hell had broken loose on the front page of the latest issue of the *Aiken Standard.* "Lynching of Longs Condemned by Ku Klux. Gov. McCormick Won't 'Pass Buck' in Lynching Probe," one headline read. "Lynching Probe Is Pure Bunk," declared another that ran above a letter to the editor from Col. Edward A. Wyman. "All this investigation and hullabaloo about who did the lynching and whys and wherefores is pure, unadulterated bunk," the colonel sneered. "The *New York World,* the Governor, the so-called 'law and order' citizens, and many others know, or could easily know, at least some of those who participated in the killing of the Longs, and know, as well as the balance of the world knows, that nobody is going to be punished and nobody wants anybody punished."

"The *World's* 'Investigation' Resented in South Carolina," read the largest headline. Barrett appreciated the mockery of the quotation marks, the way the whole article was larded with derision. He would have the public regard him as a heroic journalistic investigator, the story said, when his only apparent purpose in writing was to ridicule Aiken citizens. Actually, the article continued, *he* was the ridiculous one, for reporting that he had been warned by J. P. Gibson, the governor's investigator, that the Klan might try to usher him out of town. "About the only danger that Mr. Barrett need apprehend," the newspaper scoffed, was on the streets of Columbia, where he was in danger of "being accidentally run down by a jitney or a truck or a wild automobile driver if he attempts to cross the streets with any great degree of dependence upon the observance of the traffic signals."

And who were the "Famous Seventeen," the supposed perpetrators of the crime that Barrett referred to in every article? Did he mean to suggest that the whole mob consisted of seventeen members or that there were seventeen leaders? Was it possible, the paper suggested, "that he might have been confused by oft-repeated references to the famous 'committee of seventeen' that was going to revise the tax laws of the State?"

"Fair enough," he thought, and he laughed out loud, causing several men at nearby tables to frown at him. He could take a punch, and the madder people got, the greater the chance they'd slip up and say more than they meant to. He knew what happened to people under duress, what fell away or was stripped from them, what they might say or do. When he'd cut most of the meat off the chop, he picked up the bone and nibbled at the rest, working up the list of whom he'd visit today. Why not Colonel Wyman himself? Or maybe he'd drop in on Howard Aimar. Provoking them was his job; he did it well, and he wasn't afraid, or if he was, he knew how to control the fear so it didn't show.

But something on that page should have made him put down the chop bone and study the biggest headline again—"The *World's* 'Investigation' Resented in South Carolina." It was the word *resented* that should have focused and cleared his mind. Southern crimes and conditions—the more lurid the better—had been one of the *World's* favorite subjects. Educating himself on the state's history before he came down to South Carolina, he would have read his paper's 1907 series on the Klan. He would have found the stories about the 1903 murder of Narciso Gonzales, editor of the *State,* shot down on the street two blocks from the capitol by Lieutenant Governor James Tillman, nephew of Pitchfork Ben, who "resented" the newspaperman's articles, which Tillman believed had cost him the governorship. He would have read how, during Tillman's trial, his allies and kin had smuggled shotguns into the courtroom under their coats, in case the law failed them.

Granted, those were more primitive times in South Carolina, but not by much, and if Barrett had been raised in the state, he would have known what he was up against. He would have been schooled in resentment as thoroughly as South Carolina's children were taught the real causes of the Civil War. He would have eaten and breathed and drunk those lessons until an instinctive understanding of resentment and where it inevitably led would have been mixed with his blood and rooted in the marrow of his bones. He would have grasped that nothing was more profoundly resented here than an attack on a man's honor and standing in the community. He would have known that a man's good name was sacred; to damage it was a violent act and that, once damaged, a man's standing could only be restored by retribution, a righteous, Old Testament exchange of violence. And Barrett hadn't sullied one person; he'd attacked an entire community.

He threw two dollars onto the table and walked out of the dining room and up Park Avenue toward the courthouse. He'd start with Aubrey Timmerman again, try to goad him into saying something unguarded. He liked for the sheriff to slap him on the back, say, "Come on in the house, Mr. Barrett, since you're going to anyway." He liked to shake the sheriff's injured hand and try to make him to wince and know that he wouldn't. They understood that much about one other.

Outside the day was humid and hazy, warm for mid-November, and as he walked along, sweating, the wrongness of the weather made him uneasy. There was something unnatural about the warm, thick air and the milky light. On days like these, he felt as though he were living in the same low-pressure system of the spirit that he'd dropped into as he'd traveled south on the train. In front of the courthouse he mopped the back of his neck with a handkerchief and watched Grady Jenkins talk to the horses and mules tied to the railing there. He was working up a story in his mind about Grady, the man with eyes blank as the sky and a perfect hoofprint in the middle of his forehead, who came to the courthouse nearly every morning and stayed until the sun went down. All day he stroked the noses of the horses and mules, whispered into their ears. He pulled grass from the lawn and laid it in front of the animals then squatted to watch them chew.

When Barrett walked up, the loiterers on the benches that lined the front walk stopped talking and shouting advice to Grady. "Come to look after your brother?" the smallest man called out.

It drove Barrett crazy to think that he and Grady Jenkins were the only two people in town who didn't know who had done what on the night the Longs were killed. "Any of you men like to make a statement, now's your chance," he said.

That night he made one concession to the Klan's threat to usher him out of town: He moved his worktable away from the window of his hotel room. Then he sat down at his typewriter. "Even more bitter against this newspaper and its reporter was the group lounging in the courthouse today," he wrote. "The spokesman was a small man of vehement manner in a gray hat who thundered abuse. His confidence was that 'any twelve men in Aiken County will convict the lynchers if they are caught,' and his belief was that the World was actuated by a desire to 'put the Negroes above white men.'

"'Damn the Negroes, I say,' he offered. In 1876 we had Negroes in the Legislature. Now they know their place and they won't forget it, not here. The only reason all those lies are being published about us up North is because we're in the South.'

"The little man with the loud voice bellowed that he and all the rest of Aiken County have full confidence in the Sheriff and that the latter is doing all he can. Whereat his companions of the Court House corridor murmured their approval. But none, little man, unshaven and indignant deputy sheriff, or their companions, would give their names.

"'I am,' said the little man proudly, 'a member of the Klan.' He concluded the conversation with: 'I won't tell you a damn thing.'

"This reporter restrained his tears."

He wired the story to New York, and Swope wired back: "Cutting last line. No need to taunt." But Barrett thought of the Klan's boast that they'd tapped the telegraph wires and knew every word that passed between him and his editor. "STET, Swope," he wired back. "Enemy in sight."

After that article appeared, the calls started. The first came just after three on a Sunday morning—he noted the time on the bedside clock, in case it mattered later. Then he got up and crossed the room to the little telephone stand beside the door, holding his hands in front of him in the dark to keep from colliding with the armchair or the lamp. He picked up the heavy receiver and listened. On the other end of the line someone breathed. He held his breath, listened to the silence the way he listened to words, trying to catch the meaning.

The caller's breathing sounded ragged, and there was a hitch at the top of every inhale. Barrett stood with his eyes closed, listening. The sound could have come from the pompous man who'd told him that real leadership was what had been shown at Aiken the night the Longs were killed. He nudged back the curtain and looked out onto the empty street. One name came clearly to mind, but he didn't voice it. "Okay, pal, well, fuck you then," he said and heard a gasp before he dropped the receiver back into the cradle. So the caller was pious, but weren't they all?

In the morning, the church bells woke him, and he dressed and knotted his tie roughly in front of the mirror on the chifforobe door, unsettled by the call and what had happened later. A line from a hymn drifted through his mind: "Ye who are weary, come home." He was not weary, and he had no home. He'd lost faith in the idea of home in a bombed-out church back of the lines at Château Thierry, where they'd brought the mangled wounded and the men who'd been charred by the German flamethrowers. A large gilt-framed painting of Christ ascending into heaven had hung on the church's one standing wall. His white robes billowed around him, and he rose serenely through a clear blue sky; the wounds on his hands and feet looked small and bloodless.

For three days Barrett had worked among the wounded and stacked the dead, and every night as he lay on the ground and watched Christ rise, he felt something like heat leave his body until, after the third night, no matter how close he stood to one of the fires that was always burning, no matter how many coats he took from the pile that had been stripped from the dead, he couldn't get warm. Finally, when they'd run out of pews to burn, a man had climbed up, pulled the painting down, and thrown it on the fire, and he'd cheered with the rest of them to see it burn. Before last night he would have said that he didn't have any more faith to lose.

He went down to breakfast and found himself alone in the dining room, the only person in town, besides the kitchen help and J. P. Gibson, who wasn't at church. He sat at his table by the window, and after Helen filled his coffee cup, he nodded to show that he was ready for his food. He no longer needed to order breakfast; the help all knew him now and what he wanted: coffee first then two strips of bacon and a fried egg served on top of the grits. He almost always left a quarter on the tablecloth next to his plate. Sometimes he left fifty cents or a dollar, thought of it as payment on a long-standing debt.

The door between the dining room and kitchen swung open, and from back in the kitchen he heard loud voices. When Helen returned with his plate, he said, "Is Zeke Settles in there, Helen?"

She was young and broad and dark, and she wore her crimped and oiled hair parted on one side. He tried to catch her eye, but she looked at the floor as she refilled his coffee. "Look like he might have been here a little while back, Mr. Barrett," she said.

"If he is, send him out here, would you?" He watched her walk away, finished his meal, and lit a cigarette. The door swung open again, and Zeke sauntered through. He wore a blinding white shirt tucked into wide gray trousers held up with a skinny white belt. His small fedora was cocked at its usual angle. Miss Clara, the dining room manager, stopped in the doorway and frowned at Zeke, and though he didn't let on that he'd seen her, he took off his hat.

Late last night, after the call, Zeke had come to the door of Barrett's room. He wouldn't say what he wanted, only that Barrett must come with him, and so he'd followed him down a cramped flight of stairs and through the kitchen and out into the dark, back to where Zeke's wagon was hidden under the low, spreading limbs of a water oak. By the light of a kitchen match that trembled in Zeke's hand, Barrett had looked at what Zeke showed him. When he started to speak, Barrett hushed him. He knew what was on the shoes that Zeke had drawn out of the burlap sack. When you've seen enough of it splashed on rocks, pooled on the ground, dried on flesh and cloth, when your face has been spattered and your arms have been wet with it past the elbows, you know the look and feel of human blood. But if Zeke remembered the way he'd nodded once at the name Barrett spoke, he gave no sign. He stood beside the table with his arms behind his back and looked at a spot just over Barrett's head. "How are you this morning, Mr. Barrett?"

"You're looking sharp."

Zeke looked down at his clothes and shrugged. "Yes, sir."

"Do you work on Sunday?"

Zeke glanced down at him as though trying to figure what was being asked of him. "Depends," he said, looking away. He'd made it clear early on that he didn't deliver whiskey on Sunday or carry laundry to or from his mother. "I'm fixing to take Mama to church, then I'm going over and help Miz Libba with her flower show."

"How about I give you two dollars to drive me over to Augusta in this car I've gotten my hands on and wait while I see to some business there and drive me back?"

What Zeke had showed him last night had gotten to him more than he'd realized; he was feeling edgy again, and restless, and he knew the cure for both conditions. A plan was forming in his mind: he'd go to Augusta and look up Ella Rainey at the hotel where she'd gotten a job. "The little barefoot cotton picking bride of Horse Creek Valley," he'd called her in the article he'd written about her affidavit. He'd buy her a Coca-Cola, stir in some of Zeke's high-quality whiskey, and see what developed.

"No, sir," Zeke said. "I couldn't do that, Mr. Barrett."

"Oh, come on now," he said. "At least do me the courtesy of thinking it over before you answer."

"All right, sir. I'll do that very thing," Zeke said. He walked back across the dining room like he was in no hurry to go anywhere, setting the hat back on his head as he went. Watching him go, Barrett wondered: Why did it seem so important for Zeke to drive him to Augusta? He knew the way. Out Hayne Avenue and onto the hard-packed clay highway that ran through Horse Creek Valley, across the iron bridge over the Savannah River and into Augusta, where the Confederate soldier on his tall pedestal watched over the brick buildings and lacy balconies of Broad Street. The hotel where she'd found work making beds stood in the middle of the third block down from the monument.

He knew the way, but he wanted Zeke to drive him. He wanted Zeke to do what he'd been asked. It wasn't his fault that it was good to be a white man in Aiken, South Carolina. To act like a cock of the walk because of the color of your skin and a history that still worked in your favor, in spite of a war that had been fought to change that, and to believe that if black people no longer belonged to you, they could at least be made to feel that your goodwill was necessary to their survival. To believe that it was your natural and God-given right to expect a colored man to step off the sidewalk to let you pass, to snatch off his hat or touch the brim and call you "boss" and "captain." That it was your right and privilege to have colored women cook and clean and wash for you and do other things that white women would never lower themselves to do. To gauge whether all this was happening as it was supposed to happen with an instrument so sensitive you were instantly aware when a word or gesture was missing from the sum of humility and respect you were owed and to react as violently as if you'd been spat on or insulted and to think that living this way was a burden imposed on you by outside forces, something you never asked for or deserved.

He'd seen Zeke doff his hat to some pretty sorry-looking white men, seen him in a store, waiting to be helped until every last white person had been served. All this in a town where colored people could send their children to a good school, where there were black doctors and tailors and pharmacists and builders, John Bush at his meat market on Laurens Street, his good brass scale and his clean glass counters, his polite sons, who weighed the meat and wrapped it neatly in white paper.

It didn't take much of this kind of living to make you greedy for more; it was as hard to give up as any other thing that made you a big man in your own eyes. In the North most Negroes lived hard, but it didn't seem as necessary to an entire way of life that they be humbled. Thinking that way made him want to bring down the terrible swift sword again onto the heads of those who hadn't felt it fall the first time around.

Then Zeke was back. "I thought it over, Mr. Barrett," he said. "And I still can't drive you to Augusta."

Barrett waved him away, to show it didn't matter. "That's fine, Zeke," he said.

"But I wish you a pleasant day, sir," Zeke said.

"And yourself as well," Barrett said, ashamed of this outbreak of arrogance. What had it taken for Zeke to lead him to his wagon and open the sack, to know he could die for that and to do it anyway? Maybe he'd trusted that Barrett was not like the white men he lived among and around. Before he'd come to South Carolina, Barrett would have agreed; now he was not so sure.

12

Lewis Aimar

November 1926

L EWIS FRETTED MORE than usual that fall. His father called him a worrywart, and he was right: On any given day Lewis might be spooked by a thunderstorm, by bees or crows or mongrel dogs. He worried constantly that his mother was going to hell for being a Presbyterian. But that fall his biggest concern was the state of his father's soul. Every Saturday his father went into the booth and stayed long enough to make a serious confession. Afterward he knelt in a pew and bowed his head and closed his eyes and seemed to take his penance seriously. And yet every Sunday he stayed in the pew while Lewis received Communion. This had gone on for over a month, and Lewis knew that a Catholic avoided the Eucharist only if he had a mortal sin on his soul.

Now it was almost time for Communion again, and he knelt beside his father, feeling the worn pebbled leather cover of his father's old missal and wishing it were new. On a blank page at the front his father had written: "For my fine son Lewis, on the occasion of his First Communion." He'd hoped for a new one with crisp, gold-edged pages and a bright-red marker ribbon, not this relic with the wobbly spine and the faded marker and the gold worn completely off the pages. He shared his mother's low opinion of hand-me-downs, but his father had looked so proud when he'd handed him the gift, and he didn't want to disappoint, so he'd shaken his hand and said, "Thank you very much, Daddy." It was a sin to be ungrateful.

But his First Communion had happened on the last Sunday in

September, and now it was early November, and his father still had not bought a new missal, and that worried Lewis too. Every Sunday he whispered, "Where's your missal, Daddy?" and every Sunday his father whispered back, "I haven't had time to get a new one. I'll just look on with you." .

What was keeping his father so busy that he couldn't stop and buy a new missal from the stack of them among the rosaries and scapulars and miraculous medals in the glass case in the vestibule that the nuns unlocked after every Mass? He'd been watching his father carefully, but nothing had changed. Every morning he rousted Lewis out of bed. "Ripper-dipper and lots of pepper, give yourself a lecture," he said, and scraped his unshaven chin across Lewis's cheek. He sat at breakfast with his shirt buttoned all the way to the top, his necktie draped over the back of a chair, and ate like eating was the day's first chore. Every weekday morning he said, "Upsy-daisy," and boosted Lewis onto the seat of Zeke's wagon for the ride to St. Angela's school.   On Saturday afternoons Libba still shooed him outside to play in the yard while his father took a long nap. And every evening after supper he sat in the same light-green armchair in the front room and turned on the radio and read the paper while his mother sat in a matching chair and darned socks or read or wrote in the tall ledger book where she kept notes about the flower show. Lewis lay on the rug in front of the hearth and looked at a picture book or dozed while the warmth of the fire and the music from the radio and the sound of their two voices flowed together into a warm, slow river that he drifted on. His father had plenty of time for all those things, so it didn't make sense that he couldn't take a minute and buy a missal. But that Sunday, as usual, Lewis nudged his father and slid the old book across the top of the pew so the two of them could share.

On the top step of the altar the priest raised the gold chalice of wine, and the altar boy kneeling below reverently struck the brass bars of the small xylophone on the step in front of him: three notes up the scale, 1-2-3, a pause, then 3-2-1, another pause, then the last notes, 1-3-2. The priest whispered the words that changed the large, crisp white wafer into the Body of Christ, and when he held it up, the altar boy tapped the last three notes again. Next year, his father said, if Lewis could keep his shirt tucked in and put his shoes on properly, instead of forcing his feet into them with the laces tied and breaking down the backs, he could be an altar boy and wear a white cassock and play the xylophone at the elevation of the Host. Lewis tried not to get his hopes up because it seemed that the good things parents promised always lay ahead of you in a place you could never actually reach.

He wondered if that kind of thinking was a sin of despair. You had to be vigilant at all times, the nuns said. One little mistake, and the devil had you. He looked up and adored the Host while the priest broke it in half once then broke it again. He struck his chest and prayed three times, silently: "Lord, I am not worthy that Thou shouldst come under my roof; but only say the word, and my soul will be healed." Then he sneaked a look to see if his father was praying too. But he knelt beside Lewis, hands clenched, jaw tight, staring straight ahead the way he did when he was angry.

About *him*, Lewis thought. His father was angry at Lewis for the stunt he'd pulled before they left for church. His mother was always seeing something about him that made her want to take his picture. He looked so much like her dead brother, his namesake, or he looked exactly like his father. That morning it had been the way he'd looked in his new tweed suit and vest. "My little gentleman," she said. "Run go get the camera, Daddy." But then neither of them would let him hold his missal with the rosary looped around it, the way he wanted to; his father had ordered him to take off his cap so it wouldn't throw a shadow over his face, and finally he'd crammed the cap, the missal, and the rosary into the pockets of his jacket and stood with his hands behind his back, scowling.

Libba had refused to take the photo until Lewis emptied his pockets, and he'd dawdled and fussed about it until his father got mad and said they'd be late if she didn't go on and take the picture right now. "Just go ahead," he'd said. "Who cares about his pockets? Let him look like a ragamuffin." He knew what would happen next. When they saw the pictures, his mother would be dismayed by his expression and his bulging pockets, and his father would be put out about the money. Did she think that film packs grew on trees? And where did Lewis get the idea that he could defy his parents? After he'd been put to bed that night, he would lie on the floor with his ear to the heater vent and listen to them talk to one another in voices that he never heard them use, except at night, through the vent, about money, and know that by provoking his parents to anger, he had been an occasion of sin for both of them.

The priest stood in front of the altar, holding the gold plate piled with consecrated wafers. He nudged his father, mouthed, "Come on."

"You go," his father whispered.

Rather than disobey or argue and sin on the way to Communion, he kissed his father on the forehead and left the pew and got in the line that inched toward the altar. He folded his hands and looked down at his shoes and tried to prepare his heart and mind to receive the Host, but before he could stop himself, he began to worry about eternity. Sometimes in catechism class, after they'd each pricked a finger with a straight pin and tried to magnify that small, sharp pain into the agony our Lord had endured at His crucifixion, the nuns would make them close their eyes and imagine eternity. Given a choice between pain and eternity, he'd take the straight pin any day. Trying to imagine time without end made him queasy and panicky, as though he were falling and falling, grabbing at air as he fell. Eternity was where you went when you died, the nuns said. And whatever you found there, bliss or torment, would never end.

He was almost to the altar rail when the thought hit him like a punch to the chest: If his father died with a mortal sin on his soul, he would go to hell for eternity. The church was clear about that. Although sometimes a very good and holy person could beseech God on behalf of a sinner and God would forgive the sinner, even at the hour of his death, and whisk him to paradise. The nuns said it had been known to happen.

He checked his posture to make sure it was correct: eyes downcast, hands folded, small reverent steps. Receiving Communion properly was the first step toward becoming the person who might be able to save his father's soul, and he would offer up the rest of the day as well. He would respect his elders, provoke no one, offer no occasion of sin.

At his grandfather's house, where they always went for Sunday dinner, he pressed the doorbell four times, heard it jangle way in the back. He stood on tiptoes and looked through the thick glass of the door into the dim interior. At the end of the hall a light burned, and then someone was coming because the light came and went. And then Marie opened the door, and his grandfather was right behind her, leaning on his cane. He had a pale face and a bony nose, long white hair brushed back from a high forehead. He had bright eyes, and he always looked like he was about to tell you a big secret. "Good afternoon, young sir," he said, and Lewis bowed the way the old man had taught him—a quick dip forward with one hand held at his waist. "That's my boy," his grandfather said.

While his grandfather greeted his father and mother, Lewis ran into the parlor off the hall to wait. There were ferns on stands, heavy plum-colored drapes pulled across the windows. Where the drapes didn't quite meet, a bright strip of light pushed through. That was where he wanted to be, outside in the light and air, not trapped in here with the grownups where the talk was as heavy as the drapes.

Today, however, he would not be restless. He would wait patiently for his grandfather to come in and open the top drawer of the highboy and take out the wooden box, creak open the lid, lift the pistol out of the faded red lining, and hand it to Lewis. He would hold the pistol and listen patiently to the story of how Dr. Hastings's father, his own great-grandfather, had carried it in the war and then how Dr. Hastings had carried it at places called Hamburg and Ellenton and how one day the gun would belong to Lewis. He must honor the gun, his grandfather would say, and give it to *his* son and tell him the story and never allow the gun to leave the family. Every Sunday Dr. Hastings told this story as if Lewis had never heard it, and every Sunday Lewis had to promise to do what his grandfather asked, as though he'd never made that promise before. The story bored him. It bored the *snot* out of him, but today he would offer up the boredom and wait patiently for his grandfather to come and show the gun and tell the story.

While he waited in the parlor, he heard his father's voice in the hall. It sounded tight, the way it did when he was trying to keep his temper, the way it sounded coming through the vent. "Dr. Hastings," he said, "I would prefer if we skipped the gun today, sir."

"Now, Howard," he heard his mother say. "Why spoil it for them?"

"Haven't we all had enough of guns for a while?" his father said.

He went and stood in the parlor's wide opening, where the two heavy pocket doors had been pushed back on their tracks into the wall. He pulled them out and pushed them back with both arms, like Samson pushing down the pillars of the temple in his illustrated book of Bible stories. He did this a few times until his mother warned him with her eyes. Down the hall he watched his father turn carefully toward his mother. "Just for today, Libba, if you will indulge me, please," he said.

"No, I want to see it, really," he said. "Please show it to me, Grandfather." But that was the wrong thing to do. His father walked past him down the hall, shaking his head, unhappy with Lewis. Again.

The dining room was dim; the whole house was dim. It smelled like the clay pots stacked in his mother's greenhouse, like the cellar under his house. When he went into it, he always felt like he was holding his nose and going underwater. In the blazing summer heat the house stayed cool, which was nice, but in the winter the stuffy heat and the dimness and the heavy drapes and the hissing radiators made him drowsy. In the dining room there were more ferns on stands and a long, polished table, a tall, austere sideboard where the silver service shone on its silver tray. His father pulled out his mother's chair then sat down and spread his napkin on his lap and waited, looking as though he had a stomachache, for Dr. Hastings to say grace. He would have to try harder, Lewis thought. He would offer up his boredom and his restlessness and hope that the fragrance of his sacrifice would rise like incense to God's nose.

His grandfather spread his own napkin on his lap, folded his hands, and was about to recite the blessing when, without thinking, Lewis crossed himself. Dr. Hastings frowned at him; he didn't like to see the Sign of the Cross made at his table, and when he frowned, his thick white eyebrows bunched together, his whole face hardened. What if Dr. Hastings turned into the Roman emperor Hadrian and forbade him to make the Sign of the Cross? What if his grandfather demanded that he renounce the Catholic faith? Would he have the courage to refuse and be torn apart by lions or shot with arrows, stoned or boiled in oil or driven naked onto a frozen lake? It might be good to be a martyr, he thought, to die for your faith and cancel all your sins at once. And then he would be a saint—all the martyrs were saints. He could intercede with God on his father's behalf, and God would have to listen.

They were all looking at him: his mother signaling *Behave yourself* with her eyes, his grandfather frowning. Arms folded across his chest, his father watched as Lewis lifted his hand and moved his arm in a wide, slow, exaggerated motion—forehead, chest, left shoulder, right shoulder. "In the name of the Father, and the Son, and the Holy Ghost," he said.

Dr. Hastings pushed back his chair and stood up, his mouth gone grim. "At my own table," he said. "Shame on you." And he left the room.

Now, Lewis thought, the hour was upon him: His grandfather would come back with the old gun. He would aim it at his grandson's heart, but Lewis would spread his arms, unafraid, and welcome the bullet that would end his earthly life and save his father's immortal soul. He crossed himself slowly again. His mother looked at his father with tears in her eyes.

His father jerked him out of his chair so hard his napkin flew off of his lap. He marched Lewis down the hall and into the room where the gun stayed and pushed him down onto the maroon settee. He was as angry as Lewis had ever seen him: angrier than he'd been about the photograph, the fears, the bed-wetting, about anything. "What's gotten into you?" His father's face was very red. "What do you mean bedeviling your grandfather? Embarrassing your mother that way? Now you stay here until I tell you to come out. If I hear a peep out of you, I'll tan your hide."

After the pocket doors rumbled shut, Lewis sat on the settee the way he'd been told, while the big bag of tears inside his chest got heavier. He'd provoked his elders again, and now his soul was probably as stained and corroded as his father's. The least he could do now was to obey the letter and the spirit of the law his father had laid down.

He sat there quietly for a long time, watching the sun push through the gap in the velvet drapes. Marie bustled and sang in the kitchen, and he wished he could go sit with her and eat two pieces of cake and talk about Jesus. His mother went into the room next to the parlor and opened the upright piano and began to play "Keep the Home Fires Burning," the way she did after every Sunday dinner. If he went in, he'd find her playing quietly and singing to the photograph of his dead uncle Lewis that sat on top of the piano, as though the man with the pink lips, the yellow hair and sky blue eyes could hear her. It worried him to see her do that; he should go in there and lean against her arm to show that he was sorry. But if he went into the parlor, she might grab him and hold his chin and look into his eyes and tell him how much he looked like his uncle. Besides, he'd been banished; he didn't deserve to do any of the normal Sunday things. He deserved to sit on the scratchy settee in the stuffy room and contemplate his sinfulness.

Outside the window he heard his father's voice and his grandfather's. He got up and crept to the window and inched it open. Beyond the camellia bush that grew outside the window, he could see his father and his grandfather walking back and forth. "Somebody better watch himself," his grandfather said.

His father said, "Why tell me this?" And his grandfather said he was just saying that man better watch his step, and anyone stepping along with him should watch out too, because when you knock down a hornet's nest, what do you expect to fly out?

"He sought *me* out," his father said. "Not the other way around."

"So I've heard. I am only looking out for your best interests and the safety of my daughter and grandson. People are talking, Howard," his grandfather said.

Just then he heard his mother's light, quick footsteps coming down the hall. "And I'll tell you something else, the sheriff—" was the last thing he heard before he shut the window, ran back to the couch, and lay face down, with a pillow over his head. Was the sheriff coming to take his father? Was he going to jail, possibly to the electric chair, with a mortal sin on his soul? Lewis cried for a while then fell asleep with his cheek pressed against the wet spot on the scratchy fabric of the settee, and when he woke up, his father was carrying him. His hand pressed Lewis's head against his chest, and Lewis could hear his father's heart beating slowly, reliably, as though it would beat forever. But Lewis knew better. One of the devil's evilest tricks was to lull us into believing things were fine so we'd think we had nothing to worry about. But the nuns had taught him to be vigilant. He would have to start over again, confess and make a good Act of Contrition and double the penance the priest gave him. He would have to free his own soul from sin if he hoped to be strong enough to save his father.

13

Howard Aimar

November 1926

F IFTEEN YEARS LATER, when Lewis is about to be married, he will send his son a letter of fatherly advice. "You are taking on a big responsibility, but it is one that will make you a better man. Remember you have to be tolerant and respecting of her wishes at all times regardless. Just play the game square, and I know you will." He will mail the letter in complete confidence of the soundness of his advice, for who knew how to play a square game better than a man who had done it every day of his adult life? Who played it square all day at the office and then went home to square things with his wife? A man who would get out of bed at 10 p.m. to take the rich man's call then drive across town to the man's estate to listen while the man's wife sketched out an idea for improving the grounds.

Playing the game square was what he was doing at exactly four o'clock on November 5, 1926, when he walked through the French doors into the Highland Park Hotel ballroom, holding Lewis by the hand. Every year he paused just inside these same doors and looked down the length of the ballroom and was pleased by the orderly way the crowd moved among rows of tables arranged to place the yellow chrysanthemums next to the pink dahlias, the dahlias next to the maidenhair ferns, the red chrysanthemums, then the white. How harmonious it all looked in the light coming through three tall arched windows and showering down from the crystal chandelier in the center of the ceiling. The harmony, the beauty, the artistry, was all Libba's doing, and he admired that most of all.

Onstage a piano, drums, and guitar waited in a spotlight, and on the wall behind hung the banner: 15TH ANNUAL AIKEN FLOWER SHOW painted in green letters above a row of golden-yellow daffodils. From somewhere up front he heard Libba's bright voice, threaded through the hubbub of the crowded room. "You don't mean it," she said. "Well, aren't you sweet?" and he tracked the voice to Libba herself, in her new green velvet dress and creamy stockings, her bright mouth and dark, upswept hair. "Run go find your mother, scoot," he said to Lewis. "I'll be along directly."

He looked down the ballroom again and was pleased with the part he'd played in helping his beautiful wife make the world beautiful again. He'd paid Zeke to wax and buff the bright pine floor, to climb a ladder and wash the windows. He'd paid Minnie to wash and starch and iron the fifty heavy white tablecloths that covered the tables that held the flowers. He'd paid ten dollars to have the banner painted. Seven dollars for engraving the name of the grand prize winner on the silver tray. Fifty dollars to the band. He'd paid, and he was glad to pay; ponying up was part of playing the game square. All he asked in return was to be allowed to appreciate the beauty and harmony of the world for a few hours.

He didn't think that was asking too much. And it might have been possible if he hadn't just finished reading Barrett's story on the front page of the latest issue of the *New York World*. "Break in Ranks of Mob Is Expected Daily," the headline read, and the story beneath it was his most confident yet. "Close to a score of men stood in the little pine thicket just off the red clay road leading to Columbia and watched the three Longs die. It is the conviction of citizens and public officials that such a large number of men, implicated in varying degrees, cannot keep such a secret inviolate."

It was the idea of implication that was still wedged in his chest. Apparently, it was no longer enough to be *complicit;* now they were all *implicated.* And beyond the question of implication itself lay the issue of degree. How could you measure degrees of implication? he asked himself. How could one onlooker be more deeply involved than another? Down near the stage Lewis had found his mother. She hugged him then turned to look for Howard, and when she saw him, she kissed her fingertips and blew the kiss his way. Just then the band struck up "April Showers." The singer was a slender man in a tuxedo, a cigarette held between his thumb and forefinger, his dark hair so dense with brilliantine it reflected light. "Though April showers / May come your way," he sang.

> They bring the flowers
> That bloom in May;
> And if it's raining,
> Have no regrets;
> Because, it isn't raining rain, you know,
> It's raining violets.
> And when you see clouds
> Upon the hill,
> You soon will see crowds
> Of daffodils;
> So keep on looking for the bluebird,
> And listening for his song,
> Whenever April showers come along.

Libba stood in front of the stage, her hands clasped. *Perfect,* he could hear her say. *Heavenly.*

He started his tour at the table closest to the door that held the prize-winning blooms from every category. A blue ribbon with BEST SINGLE YELLOW CHRYSANTHEMUM printed in gold lay in front of a vase that held a spectacular six-inch bloom that looked like a small sun spreading its rays. The judges were right to choose this flower. Mr. Barrett was wrong to think of ranks. He knew it was only a figure of speech—to break ranks—but *ranks* conjured up images of order and disciplined purpose. The suffragettes had marched in ranks. In newsreels that played before the picture show during the war, ranks of our brave boys had marched against the Hun. A month after Sheriff Glover was killed, the Klan had marched in ranks down Laurens Street. But there were no ranks in the woods that night. No ranks, no plan, no one in charge, just inky darkness and shouting, the hard ribs of the field he'd stumbled across as he ran toward the crowd, hoping he wasn't too late, then the pop of pistol shots, the boom of a shotgun, and a woman's bawling screams. No ranks there, and none here now, just men he knew, men like himself, dressed in their good gray pinstripe suits and gleaming, sharp-toed shoes, who shook his hand and walked among the tables examining the prize-winning blooms, accompanied by wives like Libba in their velvet dresses and high-heeled shoes and soft, round hats.

The week before the flower show, a group of these men had decided the town needed a pep talk, and they'd chipped in for a full-page ad in the *Standard*. Three lines of heavy black type,

Tell the World
You Are Proud to Live in
AIKEN,

stacked above a drawing of a stern man slamming his fist onto a table. "Surely you have every reason in the world to be thankful you live in AIKEN," the copy read.

Compare Aiken with New York, Chicago, or any of the larger centers of the country. There it is—"Everybody for himself. Get what you can, but get it! And the devil take the hindermost." It's hustle and bustle every minute, with never a thought or a kind deed for a neighbor's welfare.

How different the spirit is here. Your neighbor's interests are your own. He thinks, "What can I do to please others? What can I do to help improve the town, help it grow, and make it a better place in which to live?" Your thoughts are the same. And through your actions AIKEN has become the best little old place in the world.

He had helped to write the copy for the ad. "How different the spirit is here," was his contribution.

At six the band began to play "Tea for Two," and the doors were opened into the adjoining dining room. Zeke lit the candles under chafing dishes that held English peas and au gratin potatoes. He stood behind the serving table, white jacket buttoned up under his chin, inspecting the blade of the long knife he'd use to carve the enormous ham in front of him. The buffet line began to move past Zeke and then Minnie, who stood next to him, ready to serve the peas and potatoes. She was dressed in her own black uniform with stiff white apron and cap. Howard moved along the serving line, adding up the money again. Every year Zeke and Minnie were paid a lump sum for setting and serving the buffet line and cleaning up afterward. This year, however, Libba had informed him that Minnie and Zeke wanted twenty dollars extra for the cleanup. "They're a team now, is that how it goes?" he'd asked Libba as he'd handed over two bills. He couldn't say exactly how it had started, but he only spoke to Minnie through Libba now, and Minnie did the same, and if Libba noticed that she'd become a go-between, she said nothing. "You tell Minnie we're square," he said. When he passed Minnie's serving station, he made sure he was talking to the man behind him in line so that all he had to do was to hold out his plate for the peas she ladled onto it.

When dinner was over, the crowd flooded back into the ballroom and stood among the flower-covered tables. The tall arched windows had filled with night and reflected the blazing chandelier. It was the moment the day had been building toward, the apex of Libba's year, when she and Howard and Lewis went onto the stage and Libba stepped up to the microphone to announce the recipients of the smaller cash prizes and finally, the grand prize winner. "Welcome, all, to the Fifteenth Annual Aiken Flower Show," she said, and everyone applauded. She touched her hair, said, "Goodness, has it been fifteen years? As many of you know, my mother started this show. As a young woman, I worked at her side, and since her passing, I have endeavored to carry on the tradition in her memory. And so life goes on, so it continues, and aren't we all grateful for this day that brings us together every year to celebrate earth's bounty as well as our deep affection for one another? And now, without further ado, I'd like to introduce my dear husband Howard, and my little man, my beloved son Lewis."

As the crowd applauded, Lewis held still, nearly rigid with importance, in his bowtie and vest, his white shirt and knickers and shiny new shoes, all bought especially for the occasion. He bowed quickly, one hand at his waist, the other behind his back, the way his grandfather had taught him. While the applause rolled on, Howard looked out at the crowd, picking out the men he sat down to lunch with on Mondays at Rotary Club, the men from the Knights of Columbus who raised their swords for the priest to walk under on his way to the altar on Christmas Eve. Were they trying to judge, as he was, to what degree they were implicated? They were all men of good character, good conscience. How had they gone to that place and stood in the dark? How had that happened to any of them?

He pulled the silver case out of his pocket, took out a cigarette and tapped it on the box, tucked it into his mouth, and lit it, without looking up. The business with the cigarette carried him through the applause, and when he looked up again, he saw Barrett leaning against the back wall, watching him. When Howard caught his eye, Barrett nodded as though he were answering a question or agreeing with Howard about something.

Behind them the band struck up "April Showers" again. Libba was about to open the envelope and call the first winner to the stage when a commotion started back near the French doors, and the sheriff and Frank Bell began to shoulder through the crowd. "Make way," he heard the sheriff say. Zeke was backing through the swinging door between the ballroom and the dining room, carrying a tray of coffee cups, and when he turned and saw them, he looked around wildly as though he might try to run, but then the sheriff grabbed one arm, and Frank Bell took the other.

By the time Howard got down the three stairs and pushed through the crowd, Barrett was there too, and the ballroom was getting quiet. Even the band had stopped playing. The piano dropped out first, then the drums. The guitar player plucked a few more notes then put down his instrument.

Howard took the tray from Zeke's hands. "What's the trouble, sheriff?"

"Nothing you need to worry about, Mr. Aimar," he said. "It's just your boy here's under arrest."

"Sheriff, I have committed no crime," Zeke said, taking care with every word.

"Be quiet, Zeke," Howard said, never looking away from the sheriff. Minnie came through the door then. He heard her gasp, and he handed her the tray of coffee cups.

"Mr. Howard, sir," Zeke said.

"Zeke, shut your mouth, and keep it shut," he said. "What's the charge, sheriff?"

"Transporting whiskey, Mr. Aimar," the sheriff said, as if the idea bored him. His big raw face was chapped, and his pale blue eyes looked watery, as though he'd just come in out of the wind. "Nothing that concerns you, I guess." Minnie staggered as though she'd been shoved; the cups slid on the tray, and Howard took her elbow to steady her. Zeke looked at her and shook his head. "Go sit down, Minnie," Howard said, but she didn't seem to hear. She stared at Zeke fiercely, as though trying to tell him something urgent with her eyes.

For weeks, for years, for the rest of Libba's life and beyond, as long as there was anyone left to tell the story, people talked about her bravery that day. Her mother would have been so proud of her, people said. In fact, many of the women who had known them both believed that the night the sheriff barged into the flower show and arrested Zeke was the night when Libba finally and fully became her mother's daughter. When the ruckus started, Lewis yelled, "Zeke!" and tried to squirm out from under her hand, but she held onto him and bent down and said something in his ear, and he stopped fidgeting and stood still. Then she held him by the shoulders in front of her, and the two of them waited as though she had perfect confidence that what was happening between her husband and the sheriff near the dining room doors had been planned and prepared for and expected, and if not, then it must be met and would be met with grace and dignity.

She turned and spoke to the bandleader, and very quietly, the men picked up their instruments and began to play "By the Light of the Silvery Moon," and Libba and Lewis stood and waited, as if they were as comfortable standing on a stage in front of the whole town while the sheriff arrested their girl's son as they would have been at home in front of the fire, as though they could wait as long as they needed to wait for this unfortunate incident to be over so that life could go back to being the way it had always been. Meanwhile, her husband and the sheriff traded angry words in voices so low no one could report with any certainty what was being said. Her husband leaned in close to speak to the sheriff, and the sheriff got in just as close to speak to him, until it seemed an afterthought that Zeke was being arrested right there in the middle of her flower show, in front of the whole town, not to mention the New York reporter, who watched it all with a self-satisfied look on his face, as though he'd finally got what he'd come for. During all that Libba stood quietly on the stage, just as her mother would have done. And never a word from her afterward about how disappointing it must have been. Never a word of complaint about how the day had been ruined. Not one.

Of course the sheriff could easily have waited, they said. He could have had the decency to arrest Zeke Settles outside the hotel, in the dark, where nobody would have been forced to watch. But you can't make a silk purse out of a sow's ear. Not that you wanted a lawman to be too silky; the job was rough, and it took a rough man to do it right. Still, the way Aubrey Timmerman bulled into the hotel ballroom that night was crude and uncalled for. But what did you expect?

As he hustled Zeke out, the sheriff made clear that his mind was made up: He was keeping Zeke in jail overnight; no need for Howard to come down and try and talk him out of it. "Me and old Zeke's got a lot to hash out," he said, looking directly at Howard, and Howard knew he'd been warned. Everybody in town knew that Aubrey Timmerman had a special relationship with the law; he used it as he saw fit. Now, with the governor promising indictments and Barrett and Wesley Barton baying like the hounds of hell after the witnesses and perpetrators, the sheriff had to be everywhere at once, swinging the law like a cudgel against anyone who might implicate him. He'd made other moves lately: permits revoked; a man threatened with a loitering citation for standing in front of the courthouse for half an hour; a flurry of liquor raids, followed by pictures in the *State* of Aubrey Timmerman, ax in hand, standing beside a chopped-up steamer outfit while a deputy poured the product onto the sand.

Minnie sat down heavily in a chair next to the kitchen door, still holding the tray of coffee cups. Her face looked ashy. "I'll be down to get you first thing in the morning," Howard said to Zeke.

"Come as soon as you can, Mr. Aimar," Zeke said.

He put his hand on Zeke's shoulder, felt it tremble. "I said I would, and I will."

But what the sheriff didn't understand, Howard thought as he trotted back up the steps and crossed the stage and took Libba's arm, what he hadn't counted on, was that Howard Aimar would not be threatened or bullied, nor would he stand for anyone under his care and protection to be bullied. The only way to deal with a man like Aubrey Timmerman was to bare your teeth and get your hackles up, shove him as hard as he'd shoved you.

The article on the front page of the next day's *Aiken Standard* called the flower show a signal success, and of course it mentioned nothing about Zeke's arrest. At the top of the front page was a three-column picture of the Aimars and the grand prize winner, holding up her silver tray. In the photograph Libba and Lewis smile, but Howard is a blur, hurrying off like a man who's late for an appointment.

14

Howard Aimar and Curtis N. R. Barrett

November 1926

THE FULL MOON had risen into the clear night sky, and its light made the pine needles gleam and turned the sandy ground to snow. Under the porte cochere outside the Highland Park Hotel, Howard walked Libba toward a cream-colored Ford touring car where Libba's cousin Lawton Hastings and his wife waited to take Libba and Lewis to their farm near Edgefield for a few days of pampering and rest, as they did every year after the flower show. Minnie followed, holding Lewis by the hand. A few minutes earlier Lawton had said he was *honored* to be taking Libba out of this unfortunate situation. Everyone was honored to do something for Libba, as though what they did for her now might make up for the humiliation she'd suffered when the sheriff barged into the flower show and arrested Minnie's son and almost got into a fistfight with her husband. In spite of the rebuke implied by Lawton's remark, Howard thought it might be good for his wife and son to be out of the picture; it would give him time and space to act on the plans he was making.

"Say, will you look at that moon?" Howard said.

Libba glanced up. "Beautiful," she said, and she turned and spoke over her shoulder to Minnie and Lewis. "Just look what a beautiful evening it's turned out to be." Lewis did as he was told, his face slack with exhaustion and dismay, but Minnie watched Howard, her eyes hard and flat. He knew that Libba was just doing what was expected of her, going through the motions. He heard it in her voice, felt it in the way her hand rested on his arm. Usually when they walked together, she took his arm and held it, but tonight, coming out of the front door of the hotel, he'd had to pick up her hand and tuck it through his elbow, and even now her hand felt too light. He knew that she was thinking about Zeke and about Minnie's fainting spell. At the end of the night he'd found Libba sitting on the hotel kitchen floor in her good velvet dress, fanning Minnie with a dish towel.

When they reached the car, Howard turned Libba to face him, leaned in close. They were not to wait up for him, he said. "Don't wait for me to come see you off. Just put your bags in the car and get going," he said. "I don't want you all out on the road too late." She nodded quickly, smiled up at him. Her lipstick had worn off, and she hadn't replaced it. She blamed him for Zeke's arrest; she and Minnie both did; he could tell by the pinched look of her cheeks and the set of her mouth. "I'm sorry, Libba," he said. "I'll bail Zeke out first thing in the morning," he said. "Tell Minnie."

"But where are you going, Howard? Why aren't you coming home with us?"

"There's something I need to do at the office," he said. "And I don't want to hold you all up."

"Maybe I shouldn't go at all."

"Of course you should go," he said. "Go and enjoy yourself, and don't worry about me. Don't worry about anything."

She looked at him steadily, waiting for more, and when it didn't come, she gave him a small bleak smile. "I don't know what to believe anymore," she said. "Get in this car with me, Minnie." The two of them climbed in and Howard closed the door, and Minnie pulled Lewis onto her lap. Howard tapped the glass, and Libba smiled and toodled her fingers at him; the fox fur on her coat collar stirred around her face. The three of them looked so warm inside the car, and he remembered what a man had written in the paper about the Aiken men implicated in the murders: "They will live and die knowing full well that they are not worthy to associate with their wives and children." He was not a murderer, so why did he feel condemned to stand outside in the cold, looking into the warm life that once was his and now was not?

Barrett answered the door with his suspenders down, shirttail out, sleeves rolled past his elbows, his face as flushed as though he'd been doing something strenuous. "Yes, sir, what can I do for you?" His voice echoed down the hall. Over Barrett's shoulder Howard saw socks on the radiator, an undershirt draped across the back of a chair. A typewriter on a small table in one corner. A large domed radio tuned to dance music. Half a glass of brown whiskey was balanced on the arm of a heavy maroon chair pulled up to the window. He sits there and watches the street, Howard thought. He drinks, and he watches us pick up the papers from the depot and makes up stories about what he sees. A small life for such a high-minded man, a man with such righteous opinions.

When Howard had first come to Aiken, he'd lived in a room like this, in a boardinghouse with a palmetto outside the window that rasped and scratched against the rusty screen day and night. He'd washed out his socks and undershirts in the sink and dried them on the radiator. Above the small desk in the corner he'd tacked up a prayer card with a picture of the Holy Family printed on the front, The Husband's Daily Prayer on the back. Every morning he'd pulled out the thumbtack and taken the card down, prayed that God would make him unselfish, cheerful, trusting, thrifty, a devoted companion. Seeing Barrett's room now was like looking back into a bleak scene from his own past, and he felt sorry for the man, for being a man like he once had been.

"Mr. Barrett," he said. "Will you go somewhere with me? I have something to tell you."

"I'm off duty," he said. "Is this a summons or an invitation?"

"Some of both."

Barrett leaned out of the doorway, holding onto the jambs, and glanced up and down the hall. "Where are the rest of the boys?" he said. He was smiling, but his eyes were not. Soldier's eyes, Howard called them.

"No boys," he said. "I dislike a mob as much as any man."

"Damn right," Barrett said. He hauled up his suspenders, stuffed in his shirttail, pulled a topcoat over his shirt and trousers. He looked like any other man called out on a late-night errand; he looked like a man who might understand how another man could end up someplace he never meant to go.

Out past the last houses the Columbia Highway was deserted, ahead and behind. The moon was halfway up the sky now, and its light seemed immense. On either side of the road the fields of spindly cotton plants looked stunned beneath its weight. The Ford's headlights were weak, but tonight they were not needed; it was almost as bright as day. Howard coaxed the car into high gear, easing the throttle lever forward with his right hand, left foot backing off the clutch, feeling for neutral, until a thunk told him he'd found the cruising gear, and the engine turned over so slowly it barely made a sound.

"You saw Zeke at the jail?" he said.

"I did." Barrett sat up straight at the edge of the passenger seat, hands braced on his knees. "The sheriff was treating him like a special guest."

"That was for your benefit," he said, felt Barrett studying him. "Like arresting Zeke was for mine. Count on Aubrey to put on a good show as long as he's got an audience. Only this time it was more than a show: He insulted my wife."

"Some show," Barrett said.

"Don't you want to know where we're going?"

"I guess I'll find out soon enough," Barrett said, but he turned in his seat to study the deserted road behind them, as though trying to memorize the way. Then he sat back. The high whine of the tires and the creaking of the suspension were the only sounds. He pulled a silver flask from his coat pocket. "You mind?"

"Help yourself," Howard said. "As you're no doubt aware, Aubrey takes a special interest in hounding people about every aspect of the whiskey business. You might call it his personal crusade, though drinking itself seems a petty crime, or no crime at all, compared to others."

"Murder, for example."

"Correct."

When Barrett offered the flask, he took it. The whiskey felt bright and warm going down. It had an aftertaste like resin, the same as the whiskey that flowed from the oak cask he kept locked in the shed over by the icehouse. The familiar taste made him uneasy, but he certainly had no monopoly on the casks smuggled into town from the river. Other men had their Zekes to haul contraband for them. "You must have a good source," he said.

"The best," Barrett said, toasting Howard with the flask. "I admire your skill with this automobile," he said. "I've heard that driving a Model T is like doing the Charleston while loading a musket after a big night at the speakeasy."

"That about covers it," Howard said.

The night of the murders there had been no need to ask for directions; he'd only had to join the line of cars traveling north up the Columbia Highway, look for the big sweet gum where the man set up his apple stand every fall, and turn there onto a narrow dirt track that ran up the edge of a played-out cotton field and into a stand of pines.

"I thought this was where we'd end up," Barrett said quietly, when the sweet gum came into view.

"You've been here before?"

"Once or twice," Barrett said, sipping from the flask. "Never had a guided tour, though." He laughed.

A guided tour. His sarcasm was unnerving, as if someone had once offered him a *guided tour,* and he was repeating those words to show how rotten they sounded. Howard was grateful to be occupied with slowing the car, making the turn. With his right hand he eased back the throttle lever, while his left foot pressed the clutch toward neutral, and when the gear shifted, he stepped on the brake pedal with his right, swung wide, and shoved the throttle lever forward again.

The track was heavily rutted from all the buggies and wagons and cars that had driven up there. He steered the Ford along the ruts, easing the throttle forward, until he came around behind the dense stand of tall pines. Then he pulled back on the left-hand lever, killed the spark to the plugs, and the engine shut down. The pine needles gleamed in the moonlight, the ground was dappled with light and shadow, and the trees threw their long shadows across the sand. The cicadas waxed and waned, and a breeze moved through the tops of the pines with a faint rushing sound.

"Do you carry a gun, Mr. Aimar?" Barrett said, looking as thoughtful as if he'd asked Howard about his philosophy of life. He sat loosely at the edge of the seat, the flask held between his legs, looking through the windshield at something far away. Howard thought he might parse for the man the distinction he'd made for himself after that night between *owning* a gun and *carrying* one. "I *own* a .38," he'd say. "I keep it in a box way up on a high shelf on the back wall of the shed where I park the car, but I don't *carry* it." But saying that might lead to more questions about motive and will and intent. It was best to answer the question as asked. "No, sir, I do not," Howard said. "Do you?"

"I was a medic in the war," Barrett said. "Medics didn't carry guns. We carried supplies to deal with what guns do. I got in the habit of not carrying one, and it stuck." He took a long pull on the flask; he seemed to be in no hurry to get out of the car.

"Let's talk *implicated*," Howard finally said. "Let's talk *degrees*."

"Let's do that."

They opened their doors and got out. "I can't tell you how dark it was that night. It was as dark then as it is light now," he said as they walked into the pines. "There were men all back in these trees, but you couldn't see a foot in front of you."

"Why is it that the story of that night always comes back to how nobody could tell up from down?"

"Because it's true," he said. He remembered blundering through the pines, holding his hands out in front of him to ward off the trees and the men who moved with him toward the torchlight in the clearing beyond and the low, angry murmur of the crowd.

He and Barrett walked out of the trees and stopped. "The crowd started here," he said, "and bent like a horseshoe around three sides of the clearing." Like the road, the ground there was churned up with footprints and hoofprints, wagon and buggy and tire tracks. He'd returned just once, the Sunday after. A crowd had milled around that day too, only this time it was made up of men and women in church clothes. Across the clearing he'd watched Aubrey Timmerman hold up his bandaged hands and tell his story. He'd been numb then, but remembering it now, he felt more certain than ever that he was right to bring Barrett here and set the record straight.

"Someone had set a lantern on this pine stump," he said. "People were yelling and running and raising so much dust, it was hard to see what was what."

"Yelling, you say? Any voices stand out?"

Howard squared his shoulders. "It was right about here that I first heard the sheriff."

Now he had Barrett's attention. He patted his coat pockets and pulled out a small notebook and a pencil stub. "You heard the sheriff yelling?" he said.

"Yes," he said. *You're in it now, aren't you, Aubrey?* he thought. *You're a big man, until you're not, until someone steps in your way and says, "Stop, in the name of the law."*

Barrett nodded. "All right," he said, and he brought the notebook close to his face and wrote something down. "Where were you when the shooting started?"

"Back in the crowd, somewhere along in here," he said, gesturing around him. The moon had cleared the trees now and hung, huge and bright, in the sky. "Why does it matter where I was?"

Barrett shrugged. "The sheriff seems to think you were— " He flipped back a few pages in his notebook: ". . . *close around,* yourself."

So Aubrey had been talking, insinuating. "Well, he would know," he said. "The crowd ended about here," he said. "I had worked my way to the middle of it when the shooting started."

It came back to him now with startling force. The boom of the shotgun, the pop of pistol shots; the way he'd been pressed against the back of the man in front of him, pushed by the man behind as they surged forward as though they'd become one thing, a thing that opened its mouth and made a sound between a shout and a groan.

After the shooting stopped and the echo sheered off through the trees, he started moving forward again, but his mind was blank, and it stayed blank until he got to the front of the crowd, where the men with torches stood, and he could see the boys lying in their blood, hear the sounds that the woman was making. "She was all shot up, but she was still alive," he said. "She was crawling on the ground with her dress on fire, and someone came up behind me and put a pistol in my hand. 'Go on,' he said. "And when I didn't, he took it back and shot her dead. At my feet," he said. "Someone shot her dead at my feet." He wanted to tell Barrett how it had been to see a woman killed and to try and apply the words that had been spoken in the lawyer's office that day—*justice* and *the righting of wrongs*—to the mayhem and carnage of that moment. But Barrett wanted something else.

"By 'someone,'" he said, "you mean the sheriff?" His pencil was moving, but he watched Howard as he wrote, as if he were drawing him.

Then, just as clearly as if he were lifting the newspaper from a bundle on the platform down at the depot, he saw the headline: "Witness Hints He Knows Who Fired Fatal Shot." *An eyewitness account by a prominent local businessman,* Barrett would call what Howard had told him, and the sheriff would fill in the rest. And then what the sheriff had begun and he had come here to finish would start again. Resentment and revenge, revenge and resentment: a big wheel turning, carrying him and the sheriff through battle after battle until both were dead; turning long after they were dead if they'd tied their children to it. He thought of Lewis, chained to that wheel until the wrong the sheriff had done his father was finally avenged. "It was dark," he said. "There was a big crowd, and it was dark. There were guns all through that crowd. It could have been anybody."

Barrett made a disgusted noise low in his throat. "So you hauled me out here to tell me that it was dark?" he said. "God Almighty, damn." He shook his head, spat on the ground. "Or did you mean to tell me that it was you who shot her dead?"

"No," he said. "I told you, someone took the gun away."

"Which brings us back to the sheriff."

"It could have been anybody. I did not turn around."

"Too dark to tell one buzzard from the other?" Barrett said.

"If that's how you want to look at it." He wouldn't be provoked.

"What a waste," Barrett said. "What an insult to the memory of thousands of men whose killers will never be known not to name killers who can be, and are. So tell me again, what exactly did you do that night?"

"Nothing," Howard said. "God help me. I did nothing."

And then, almost as if speaking to himself, Barrett said, "So that's how you got blood on your shoes."

The breeze had stopped, and the trees stood motionless; their long, straight shadows fell across the clearing. Howard heard the rasping pulse of cicadas and, from somewhere far away, the baying of hounds. He saw himself from far away too, and he imagined he had a gun in his hand. He raised it and fired, and Barrett fell and lay as still and empty as any of the dead; an emptiness so complete that once you saw it on a human face, you could never again believe that death was anything but oblivion.

He imagined himself driving back to town, setting the gun on Aubrey Timmerman's desk, and telling him what he'd done. At his trial he would claim self-defense. "If killing Curtis N. R. Barrett was evil," he would say, "it was a necessary evil, committed in defense of a marriage, a family, a community, a way of life." No jury of his peers would convict him because every man among them would know what self he had been defending and why.

He would gladly have left Barrett there if the man hadn't sprinted to the car as Howard was turning around, jumped onto the running board, and pulled himself inside. As soon as they were back on the highway, Howard pushed the Ford into cruising gear. "Look here, Aimar," Barrett said, with the false heartiness of a man trying to bluff his way out of a bad situation, "what I said about your shoes was pure speculation." He waved his hand through the air, erasing the words. "I know from personal experience that if you're standing close when someone's shot, the blood finds you. See what I'm saying?"

"What kind of fool do you take me for?" Howard watched the road ahead as though he were following a trail of bloody footprints that led from his wife to Minnie. No doubt, Minnie had been given the shoes to clean and the story of the dove field to contemplate. But Minnie would have had her own story. She'd come out onto the porch of her house that morning, shading her eyes against the rising sun. And then, because there was no Zeke without Minnie, no Minnie without Zeke, the trail led straight to the boy whom he'd fed and housed and loaned money to buy his horse and wagon, the one he'd trusted to drive to the river landing and back and paid top dollar to do it and helped in every way it was possible for a white man to help a colored boy. That same boy had shown the shoes to Curtis N. R. Barrett and told the reporter what his mother had told him and given Howard a permanent place on Barrett's list of those who were up to their necks in gore, implicated to the highest degree.

15

Aubrey Timmerman

December 1926

E WAS USED to the calls from the governor's office now; he knew how to read the signs. On the good days the governor himself was on the line. "Aubrey," he'd say, with a big sigh, "need to see you again, son." On those days the sheriff could relax, because when Governor McCormick claimed him as his flesh and blood, he could count on a warm welcome at the statehouse. His Honor was a small neat man with a soft moon face and mild eyes; he perspired in every season, was forever mopping his face and neck and palms with a big monogrammed handkerchief. On the good days the governor would bustle out of his office and rest one moist hand on the sheriff's shoulder, tell his pretty secretary to bring his hardworking boy a Coca-Cola. Then they'd stroll into His Honor's office, where the windows and their green velvet drapes almost touched the ceiling and oil portraits of the men who'd gone before them into glory looked down from every wall. Wade Hampton was there, Cole Blease and John C. Calhoun and Pitchfork Ben Tillman—in profile, to hide his missing eye. To the side of the governor's desk stood three flags: Stars and Stripes on the left, the palmetto and crescent moon of South Carolina on the right, and in the center, a step in front of the others, the flag of the Confederacy. The men on the walls would have disapproved of any other ranking.

On the good days, once they'd settled themselves on opposite sides of the governor's gleaming mahogany desk, the glass of cola was brought and set down on a glass coaster in front of the sheriff, and the secretary went out, closing the tall double doors behind her.

Then Aubrey Timmerman could get down to the business of bringing the governor up to date on the progress of the investigation in Aiken County.

Early this morning, however, the pretty secretary had called and spoken to him in a crisp voice without a flicker of welcome in it: "Hold for the governor, Sheriff Timmerman." That was the sign that this would be a bad day, and he knew why.

For the last few days Gibson's blue touring car had been seen gliding up and down Laurens Street or staggering along a washboard road out in the county or nosed up to a small white house in one of the Horse Creek Valley mill villages, and this meant that a fresh batch of affidavits would soon be on their way to governor. Worst of all, two days ago Gibson's car had been parked for a solid hour in front of John Moseley's house in Graniteville, and it wasn't the first time the governor's detective had paid the old man a visit. Hearing that Gibson had visited Moseley again had made the sheriff's heart clench for a second, followed by the lighting of a deep and murderous anger at the injustice of the role the vindictive old lunatic had come to play in this business. In every corner of Moseley's haunted house of a mind, the old man kept ledgers in which he traced the strands of the web of corruption he swore was spun all over Aiken County, insinuating to Gibson, to Barrett, to anyone who would sit still long enough to hear him out, that from the lowliest jailer and chain gang guard up through the ranks of local law enforcement, the whole county was honeycombed with Klan and that the hand of the Invisible Empire had pulled the strings in the Long killings.

John Moseley knew these things because he'd once been a big shot in the Klan, back when it was the one true Klan and its stalwarts were the Red Shirt men of Hamburg and Ellenton, members of the local gentry and high-office holders whose names never appeared on any membership rolls. But then, so his account went, along came the thieves and thugs and murderers and bootleggers, the hutch dwellers and croppers, the white trash and corrupt lawmen, who drove the good men out until the Klan you had now was a rump Klan, a gang instead of an empire, lawbreakers instead of defenders of the law. The sheriff thought he might need to remind His Honor, in case he had forgotten, that two of the governor's cousins were on Leland Dawson's list; they were all in this thing together.

Waiting for the governor, the sheriff tapped a pencil on the desk, looked out the window. It was a brilliant winter day, the light as clear as water in a tall clean glass, sunlight flashing like diamonds through the dark canopy of leaves on the water oak in the yard between the courthouse and the jail. He wished he could go out into that beautiful world, tip back a chair against that old oak and take his ease; every man had the right to do that once in a while. He wished he had his old job back: steering the trolley car, collecting fares, swinging the door open and shut at every stop, sending Negroes to the rear or telling them to wait for the next car if white people had taken all the seats. Brakes and gears and rolling down the track, keeping to your timetable—that was all there was to it. The trolley ran straight as an arrow out Trolley Line Road from Aiken to Augusta, Augusta to Aiken, and looking back on it now, it seemed that he'd steered that car through a simpler world, a simpler time, where colored and white had *both* been happier. Now he rued the day he'd said, "You bet," when Bud Glover asked was he interested in becoming a lawman.

Then the governor was on the line. "Sheriff Timmerman," he said, "I will see you in my office at three this afternoon, sir."

And so, once again, the sheriff sped along the hard clay highway toward Columbia, glaring at the leftover cotton bolls on the brown plants in the fields beside the road as if they'd sworn affidavits against him too. He'd gotten wind of the latest batch of documents; he still had friends who wished him well and wanted him to stay out in front of what was coming at him, like Ella Rainey's latest contribution to the public good.

"Sheriff Timmerman came up and asked did I know any of the people who had taken the Negroes. Just the sheriff and Bates, I said. I did not tell him I knew Smith and Gaddis. He turned pale as a ghost and said it wasn't him I'd seen. I told him that he was the only sheriff I knew. He said it wasn't him, and he left."

He drove on through the drab endless fields, rehearsing how he'd respectfully ask the governor to recall that he'd risked his life one time to save those three on the night Earl Glover was killed; he didn't see how he could have been expected to do it twice for three murderers who were guilty as sin.

"Later jailer Bates brought our supper. I asked him if one of the Longs came clear, and he said, 'Yes, but probably not for long.' Before this I saw Sheriff Timmerman and State Constable Gaddis talking out in the yard. Mr. Gaddis started to walk off, and Sheriff Timmerman said, 'We will finish this case tonight.' I heard this as I was laying in the window."

Laying in the window. That detail right there should tell His Honor something about the credibility of the affidavit swearers that J. P. Gibson had flushed from cover this time. He drove on toward Columbia, building his case. On the night in question, he'd say, maybe he did make some errors in judgment; he'd admitted as much on a previous visit. He'd even allowed that he was as angry as any other citizen about the possibility that those three might waltz away scot-free. This time he would put a bigger question to Governor McCormick: If Aubrey Timmerman was the cold-blooded man those affidavits made him out to be, why did he scorch his hands beating out the fire in a dead colored girl's dress? He would hold out his hands to the governor again, let the welts and the new pink skin plead his case. No sir, he'd say, he didn't mind one bit going over the story again; in fact, he welcomed the opportunity because every time he told it, he remembered more details that made the whole picture sharper.

In their affidavits all those people claimed that they'd heard him on the stairs. Fair enough, goddamnit, he'd say; they did. He was man enough to own up to a moment of irresolution. He'd started up, yes sir, then went back down. "But let me ask you something as one Christian man to another," he'd say. "Can't a man's moment of weakness be redeemed by a later show of strength? Isn't redemption just about the whole message taught by our Lord's life, death, and resurrection?"

"Then the cage door rattled and in a few minutes the lever clicked and the door flew open. 'What are you going to do with that cigar box?' somebody asked. And the Long boy said, 'I'm going to carry it home.' And another man said, 'You don't need that damn thing,' and I heard it hit the floor about that time. In a few minutes I heard the girl, Bessie Long, yell: 'Lord have mercy,' she said. 'What you all going to do with me?' In a few minutes I heard the automobiles go off and the Longs hollering as far as I could hear. I did not hear any scuffling in the jail. Nobody pulled the cover off my head, I was wrapped up in it too far."

Jailbirds with their heads under the covers. Window layers. The little whore Ella Rainey, who'd sworn in an earlier affidavit that she'd recognized his voice and his back. Not that she couldn't identify a man by his back—she'd felt enough of them working over her to know the look and feel of one. He drove down the last hill and onto the Broad River bridge. An early-morning mist had risen from the river, and halfway across the bridge he drove into a patch of that fog and felt a glum weariness descend. He was sick of this business, sick of what people had been saying about him from the minute he was sworn in as sheriff, maybe for his whole life. He remembered old Dr. Hastings's wife standing in the door of their house close beside the Graniteville Mill, a Christmas basket in her hand. She'd worn a dark cape trimmed in fur, combs in her hair. He hadn't forgotten what she wrote in the Aiken paper about her club's work among the hutch dwellers in Horse Creek Valley: "the least of our brethren."

That was the stink of family, the birth slime that never washed off. Then there was the other stink, caused and fanned by his many enemies who never wanted him to be sheriff because of the goods he had on them. What he knew about where and how Ella Rainey's brothers made their whiskey and who they sold it to was reason enough for her to lie about him. All he would be trying to say was that a lot of people followed Aubrey Timmerman like buzzards looking for a chance to swoop in and tear another piece of flesh from his long-suffering carcass.

He could remind the governor of all those facts and circumstances and histories, rearrange the pieces of the story of that night a hundred times and still be left with one that would not fit, and that was the moment they'd brought Bessie Long down the metal steps from the second-floor cages, cursing and screaming and grabbing at everything in sight. She was a big strong woman, and at the bottom of the steps she'd grabbed a doorjamb and held on tight. They'd shouted and yanked her hands while she screamed and twisted and fought them and held on until he'd thought she was going to rip the jamb clear off the door. The men holding him had pinned his arms, but he'd been close enough to speak to her. "Hush, girl," he'd said. "They're going to carry you home." She'd let go of the doorjamb then and grabbed at him with her eyes like he was her blessed Lord, and she was still looking to him to save her when they'd dragged her away. And to this day it would not come clear if he'd meant his words to comfort or deceive.

All that month he went to Columbia when he was summoned; he drank a Coke with the governor, or he didn't; he told his story again, added and subtracted from it, trimmed and shaded and colored it, and the governor dithered and stalled his way to the end of his term in office. "Governor Passes Buck," read a December headline in the *State,* but Arthur McCormick waved away the insult as he would a gnat. He was a Christian, he said, and the Lord knew his heart. Pressed for comment, he repeated a favorite saying: "Sticks and stones may break my bones, but words will never hurt me." Especially when those words came out of people's mouths and buzzed around like flies that never actually lit on anything that could be proved true.

So Aubrey Timmerman sat tight, and he advised everyone who sought his counsel to sit tight, and sure enough, just before Christmas, Curtis N. R. Barrett wrote one final article for his New York newspaper in which he claimed that the era of lynch law was just about over in the South. Then he packed up his fancy shirts and his silver cuff links, his cigarette case and his flask, his bag of insinuation and innuendo and character assassination and contempt, and slunk back to New York City, where he swore that what had happened in Aiken, South Carolina, was the damnedest thing he'd ever seen, and he'd seen a lot, both in the war and after.

When the sheriff heard that Curtis N. R. Barrett had vamoosed, he wished like hell that someone had told him the man was leaving; he would have run to the depot to see him off. He would have whipped out his pocket handkerchief and waved it like crazy until the ass-end of that northbound train had rattled out of sight. Then, sure enough, in January 1927, as Aubrey had prophesied, the Aiken County Grand Jury was seated one more time to take up the Long killings. They examined the eighteen affidavits that J. P. Gibson had collected. They questioned the people who'd given them, and they ruled once and for all that there was insufficient evidence to hand down any indictments, and finally, *finally*, it was over. Aubrey Timmerman's name had been cleared, or at least nothing he'd claimed to be true had been proven in a court of law to be false, and that was good enough to allow him to keep his job and to earn for him, a few years later, a position as an Internal Revenue Service officer and, a few years after that, a picture and a brief biography in a book called *Ninety Years in Aiken County.*

16

Howard Aimar

June 1943

"WAIT," HE SAYS, but the priest kisses and folds his purple stole; he slips the chalice back into a linen bag, zips shut the case of Communion wafers, and packs everything away in his black leather satchel. "I gave the general absolution," he says. "Our God is a merciful God." But Cecile weeps into her hands because it's her fault the priest came too late to hear her father's last confession. She was blinded by pride in her own judgment that there was still time, and she waited too long to call. He hears the priest and Libba trying to console her, and he wishes he could console her too. "It's all right, Cecile," he wants to say. "You've done nothing wrong. Hope blinded you. Where's the sin in that?"

Then Libba sits on the bed, presses her warm body against his, kisses his mouth. "Darling," she whispers. "My love." She speaks from the place he's steadily, slowly drifting away from, down and down. He needs to tell her that the room is too crowded; some of these people must go. Lewis's daughter seems permanently installed in a chair beside his bed—nothing can be done about that—but the others must leave now. The ones who stand in the corners and gather around the bed with their heads bowed so he can't see their faces or know their names. Their voices flow around him and pull at him like the current in the floodwaters he'd once walked through.

At least Lewis's daughter isn't afraid to show her face, and looking at her, he feels an urgent need to tell her about the day the Savannah River spilled into Augusta and he walked home through the flooding streets. At first, he tells her, the water was up just over the soles of his shoes, and it was lively fun to splash through it, so much fun that he'd walked until the water lapped over his ankles, before it occurred to him that he'd better go home. By the time he turned onto Ellis Street and saw their house, the water was up to his waist, running strong. A long pine board rushed past him, then a tree limb and a dead cat. He was just a boy, didn't know that no matter how wide it spreads, a river moves toward the sea. Half a block from home he found it hard to walk. The current kept sweeping his feet out from under him, trying to carry him where it was going, and he remembered the dead cat and knew that it made no difference to the water whether he swam or floated, struggled or sank. At their house the water was rushing over the fourth step, curling back in small waves from the bars in the stair railing. He'd had to grab onto a baluster to haul himself out of the current.

All his life, he says, he has felt like that boy clinging to the baluster, trying not to be swept away. He does not know why he told her that last part—he has never told anyone else—but now she's crying, and her tears are not entirely unsatisfying. *She is sorry,* she says, taking his hand, *sorry that he'd had to pull himself out of the water. Someone should have been there to help him,* she says. *No child should have to feel alone and afraid like that.*

"Yes, well," he says. "Enough whimpering. You never saw my name on any list of perpetrators of that heinous crime, and you never will," he says. "I swore no affidavit. I am never quoted by name in a newspaper article or accused of a role in anyone's murder."

Yes, she says. *But you were there. What do you call those who stand in a crowd and watch three murders? Are they onlookers? Bystanders? Witnesses? What do you call people who know and do not speak? What do they call themselves? I need to know.*

"Why? Who made you a judge? What gives you the right?"

Because you are mine and I am yours, she says. *I need to know what to call myself.*

An image flares in his mind, an illustration in a book about the ancient tribes of the South Carolina coast who stripped the flesh from the bodies of the dead before burying them in waterlogged graves. A figure with a tattooed face and long fingernails, a high-ranking person, honored and feared. "Try Bone-picker," he says.

He has hurt her, but so be it. The truth hurts sometimes. *And you?* she says. *What do you call yourself?*

"A coward," he says. "Are you satisfied?"

That fits.

"Fits who?"

All of us.

Forgiven or unforgiven, there's something he must do. "And now, good-bye," he says. He takes back his hand from hers. The war has not begun, and so Lewis has not gone to fight in it. He has graduated from Clemson College and been sent to New York to work in the rich man's home office. A golden opportunity for his boy, and he must be a good father and write to his son. He picks up his heavy Sheaffer fountain pen, smooths down a sheet of engraved stationery. "Stick on the job," he writes, "for the time you feel you are not getting anywhere is just the time you will find out that you are clicking along in top shape."

"We don't want any criticism to come up for anything," he writes. "Cultivate that secretary's friendship, and send her or give her a box of candy or something once in a while. It is well worth it. Don't ever let them think that you're not a hard worker, and don't let anyone believe you're not for them because then they might conclude that you're against them."

Libba stands and starts for the door to look for Minnie. Cecile is done with weeping now and gone back to being her sturdy, competent self. She holds his hand, says, "Mother, where are you going? Don't go," but Libba walks briskly out into the long white hall then leans against the cool tile wall and closes her eyes. "I'm tired, Howard," she says. "I just need a minute to catch my breath." When she opens her eyes, Minnie is coming slowly toward her down the hall, tall and thin in a pale yellow dress, placing in front of her with each step a rubber-tipped wooden cane, her face a rebuke to pain. She promised she'd be here at five o'clock, and now it is close to six, but ever since that January day in 1927 when Minnie left her little cottage in their backyard and moved into her own house on Toole Hill, she comes and goes as she pleases. She has come in her own good time, and Libba shows her into Howard's room. "Miss Aimar," she says to Cecile, and she stands beside the bed leaning on her cane and looking down at Howard. "Uh, uh, uh," Minnie says, shaking her head. "You're walking that lonesome valley now, aren't you?"

"Be kind now, Minnie, he can hear you," Libba whispers. "My father said hearing is the last sense to go." Minnie turns to her and tightens her lips, draws into herself the way she does when she's deciding how big a piece of her mind she's about to give you. "Oh, don't listen to me," Libba says, pressing a hand to her forehead. "Say what you want." Minnie considers this, head bowed, before she turns back to the bed. She smells of sweet talcum powder and Octagon soap. She wears her steel-gray hair in two tight braids crossed and pinned over the top of her head, the way she's always worn it. She smooths a wrinkle out of his sheet, pats his arm, and rests her hand there for a moment. "You just keep walking, Mr. Aimar," she says. "You'll get where you're going."

Out in the hall again, Libba walks with her. "Now, Minnie, please tell me when Zeke plans to bring those grandchildren to see you? It's not right for him to do you that way. He should move back here with them so they can be close to you. New York is no place to raise children. Has he forgotten where his home is?"

"I keep up with my son, Mrs. Aimar," Minnie says. "He'll be along directly. You better go on back in that room and see about your husband."

Minnie has gone, but Zeke has stayed. He hadn't noticed him before, the room was so crowded, but now that Minnie and the priest have gone, he sees Zeke standing at the window, looking out. He'd know that slouch, that cocky hat, anywhere. "Zeke," Howard says, but Zeke doesn't turn. "You did what you had to do, and I did the same." Back in 1926 he'd had the last word, of course; that was the way things were then, the way they mostly still are now. He cannot imagine how Zeke could have thought he could betray him and walk away from that moment unharmed. Still, if Zeke had betrayed any number of other men so flagrantly, Zeke would be dead.

He comforts himself with that fact now at the hour of his death, the moment he's come to at the end of every Hail Mary. *Pray for us sinners now, and at the hour of our death.* The hour of our death. How could something as wide and full and deep as a life dwindle into a last hour, a last minute, the moment itself? The shadows of summer leaves rush across the front of his house. The singing of a yellow canary frightens him. He feels breath on his face, a voice in his ear. "My darling," Libba whispers, as if she could send those words with him out into oblivion, out into eternity and its ever-receding certainties.

17

The Curious Grandchild

IGHTY YEARS ON, what is left of the Long story are fragments, glimpses, and silence. Seen from this distance, the story makes a design full of missing pieces, but one with enough order and consequence left to allow a person to fill a gap, to hear a missing word or cry, and that is what the curious grandchild has been trying to do: imagine the missing pieces, people the silence.

She is trying her best to make this blighted story come out right, even as she asks herself what that could possibly mean. Justice for the dead? Guilt established and exposed? Maybe she wants to piece this story back together, to make it as whole and true as it can be, because she believes that stories can act as antidotes to amnesia and complacency; that telling stories is one way to remember what we're capable of doing to one another. Maybe she wants to fit the pieces together until the look and sound and smell of this story, the shadow it throws, will be so familiar she will know it when it happens again.

And what about her place in all this? After all, she's not telling a story that happened to someone else; it's a part of her own history that she's trying to reconstruct. She doesn't want to leave herself out, or her grandfather either. She doesn't want to ignore any piece that might make the design more apparent. She never knew her grandfather; he died while her father was overseas during World War II, years before she was born. He exists for her in photographs and stories told about him by others, and the man who emerges from those pictures and stories was no bigger or more noble than any other man of his time, a time in which the freest thinkers in the state—and they were few—

could not imagine a world where white supremacy was not the letter, the spirit, and the foundation of law and custom.

She wants to say how tightly he was woven into a web of family and community loyalties. His wife's father was the coroner's physician who counted Sheriff Earl Glover's wounds and wrote Bessie Long's confession on his prescription pad and saved her life. He examined the Longs' bodies and testified before two inquests. One of the men on Leland Dawson's list of perpetrators—the Famous Seventeen—sponsored her father at his Confirmation. She wants to say that the binding energies of his time and place, the physics of family and civic and racial loyalty, would not have allowed her grandfather to stay clear of a crime in which his wife's family was so deeply immersed, so personally involved. She wants to say that he was there that night, a *prominent local businessman* who witnessed the murders, or a member of the mob that dragged the Longs from the jail and drove them to the killing field, that he added his cowardly silence to the silence that came after.

She wants to say that she has been a coward too, a lesser coward but still a coward, bound by the same loyalties. There is a family photograph of a Christmas in the 1960s: aunts, uncles, cousins, in front of the festive tree at Libba's house, and in this picture the curious grandchild stands apart from her relatives with her arms folded, looking smug and pleased with herself because she's just gotten scolded for saying "Yes, ma'am" to the maid in front of her grandmother. Because she's proud that she had recently joined the Human Relations Commission, an interracial group that meets to talk justice and equality, and has conveniently forgotten or ignored or deleted the fact that she has even more recently *resigned* from the group after her father said it would hurt his business if people found out that she belonged. If that picture were taken today, maybe she would step in closer, join her kin, all of them bound to one another by their evasions and the stories they tell in their own defense as surely as they are joined by blood and shared history.

Eighty years on, and she wants to take a last look at the design.

A glimpse: As tenants farming cotton on Harley Johnson's land, the

Longs lived one rung up the shaky ladder from sharecropper. Cotton was a brutal crop. Its roots broke down humus and stripped nutrients from the topsoil so quickly and efficiently that after only a few years, a cotton field turned into a wasteland of hard clay gullies. It was also a sickly crop, constantly threatened by the boll weevil and the firebug, by spider mites and thrips, blight and gall and powdery mildew, by stem and root rot and all sorts of leaf collapse. To farm this crop they would have furnished the labor, the work animals and their feed, the tools, seed, and a portion of the fertilizer used to make the crop, and in return they were paid for the crop, minus the house rent, minus the debts at local stores and gins and mills for supplies and services. Minus, minus, minus. Tenant farmers, black and white, often got cheated outright or so tangled in webs of credit and merchant's liens that they ended the year broke or in debt to the landlord for the next year's crop before the seed was planted.

By the standards of the time Herbert Long was a successful tenant farmer. He owned mules and plows, and he had a large family to work the crop. But people make enemies. They are careless and highhanded; they take advantage of people, or they are disliked for being meek when they should be strong or strong when they should be meek, or for no good reason. And in 1925 it could be fatal for a black man in South Carolina to better himself by climbing over a white man. To better himself at all. Just before that Saturday morning in April 1925, their landlord had taken away a mule from a white tenant and given it to the Longs; he'd rented them a few more acres of land as well. One rumor going around after the sheriff was killed was that the white tenant who'd lost his mule to the Longs had told the sheriff they were selling whiskey. Or the preacher from the church closest to their house might have informed on them, for selling to his congregation, though he denied it in a letter to the *Palmetto Leader.*

And maybe the Longs did sell whiskey as a side business. Many people did. Maybe the sheriff had been watching them. A few weeks before the fatal raid, Dempsey had been dragged out of the house and whipped by a group of unknown men for unknown reasons.

"My name is Marie Long," Dempsey's sister testified at the coroner's inquest into Sheriff Earl Glover's murder.

> I am the daughter of Herbert Long.
> I am eighteen years old.
> I was there last Saturday morning.
> I was nursing the baby.
> I did not know who was the sheriff.
> I don't know how many guns were in the room.
> I don't know where Bessie, Albert, or Dempsey were.
> I don't know whether they came back to the house.
> I don't know who shot the sheriff.
> I don't know who got the gun.
> I don't know where they kept the pistol.
> I have seen a shotgun in the house.
> I haven't ever seen that knife.
> I didn't know the sheriff was dead.
> No one hadn't told me anything.
> I saw the pistols in their pockets, and that's the reason I ran.

"My name is Clara Long," reads her testimony at the inquest into the sheriff's death. "I am the wife of Son. His real name is Dempsey. Son and I live with Sam. I was at home Saturday morning when the sheriff and officers came over. When they came, I was in the kitchen. I saw the car come up. I did not know who they were. I had started to cook dinner. After while I heard a noise like somebody fussing. I heard someone shoot, and I looked around, and I said death is nothing but death, then I got my baby and jumped over the wire fence. I did not know who the sheriff was. I do not know who shot first or shot last."

It wasn't clear then; it isn't clear now; it will never be clear what happened on the day the sheriff was shot or on the night the Longs were taken from the county jail and killed. The names of the dead are the only certainties: Sheriff Earl Glover. Dempsey and Bessie and Albert Long. Mamie Long, mother to Dempsey and Bessie, aunt to Albert.

The rest is all darkness and mayhem, rancor, mystery and silence. Albert testified that when the two cars of white men pulled up in front, he and Dempsey were walking back toward the house from the field across the road. He said that Mamie Long killed the sheriff. At first Dempsey agreed, but at the trial he testified that Albert had fired the shotgun. There were rumors that Aubrey Timmerman had shot his boss because he was about to be fired, but they were squelched when Libba's father, Dr. Henderson Hastings, examined the sheriff's body and testified that the ninety-three wounds in the man's back and side had been made by a shotgun blast, and the deputies all carried pistols.

An imagined fragment: Curtis N. R. Barrett might have written down the words he'd heard the white people use to sort and rank the black people they lived among and around and, to their way of thinking, above. That sort of thing would have been interesting to him. *Negro, colored, nigra, coon, nigger,* it went, in descending order of dignity. Dr. M. M. Hampton, who ran his own private hospital, was a Negro, as were the building contractors William and Wesley Ford. The meat market proprietor John Bush was a Negro, and so was Ezra Jones, the tailor who specialized in making riding habits for the rich. There were other Negroes too: shoe repairmen and barbers, blacksmiths and wheelwrights and real estate agents.

Colored was practically synonymous with *Negro,* but *nigra* was a tricky word, balanced between the respectability of *Negro* and *nigger,* the lowest of the low. Ladies usually said *Negro* or *colored* or *nigra. Nigger* was the word that the hard little men in overalls spat onto the street, and so did the doffers and spinners and the foremen in the mills down in Horse Creek Valley, which did not hire blacks. Lawmen used it regularly, though Barrett had heard it slip out of many a white man's mouth when he was provoked or affronted. Howard Aimar and the governor had both used the word with him, one white man to another.

Within each category there was room for further nuance. *Niggers* could be good or bad, depending on the trouble they caused. On Saturday nights *bad niggers* got drunk and cut one another with knives and broken bottles in the juke joints that lined the alley behind Laurens

Street. They carried themselves with belligerent dignity and wouldn't doff their hats. And once you were a *nigger,* Barrett would surely have noted, you'd best beware. But what he never got used to was how easy it was to be consigned to that category, even if you'd been *colored* or *nigra* or *Negro* before. Albert, Dempsey, and Bessie Long had each fallen from *Negro* to *bad nigger* to the clearing in the pines where they died.

More fragments: Soon after the Long murders, a photograph of a woman appeared in the *New York News* under the caption "Bessie Long, Martyr of Aiken Mob." It shows a matronly woman with a broad mild face. A schoolteacher, you might guess. It's hard to imagine that the woman in the photograph could have wrenched a deputy's gun from his hand or torn a chunk of flesh out of Aubrey Timmerman's arm with her teeth.

In November 1926 Clara Long wrote a letter to Leland Dawson from 1537 Park Ave., in Philadelphia. "Lawyer N. R. Latham asked me to send you my peoples picture who were murdered at Aiken on the 8th of October, but I am sorry to say that I am unable to find any. My husband Dempsey Long, his sister Bessie Long and his first cousin Albert Long, all three were murdered and I would like to hear from you please."

The 1930 census lists no Longs in Aiken County, but eighty years on, the house is still there, a small, dark-red, wooden house near the Coleman Thankful Baptist Church on the east side of SC Highway 39 outside Monetta. The unmarked common grave where Bessie, Albert, and Dempsey Long are buried is somewhere nearby. The memory is still there in the mind of a distant relative whose grandmother told him the story of the Long killings. She talked about it all the time, he said. How they dragged them out of jail like dead mules. When he drives past the house, he remembers that story, and remembering it sometimes keeps him quiet when a man insults him.

The outrage is still there too; it smolders in the dozens of letters that Leland Dawson wrote to judges and lawyers, senators and ministers. It blazes in his letter to the editor of the DeLand, Florida *News.* "You ask, 'Who is to blame?' for the brutal murder of a woman and two men, one of whom had been found not guilty by the presiding judge. You further insinuate that the mob and the local sheriff were better judges of the issue of guilt or innocence than the Supreme Court of the State. You directly pose the question whether sheriffs ought to be asked to risk their lives 'in the interest of a man they know to be a criminal,' although the State declares him innocent of any crime. Your editorial is a perfect example of the state of mind which moves us to keep up the pressure for a federal law to deal with these outrages which continue to be defended and justified by editors such as yourself who pay lip service to law enforcement."

A silence, a gap, an imagined glimpse: Minnie Settles would have had her own opinion about what had happened at the Long place on that April morning. It wasn't right to kill the sheriff; killing was an abomination, a foul sin. But what was to be done, she asked herself, when two cars full of white men pull up in front of your house and the men jump out and come running, and you see the pistols in their pockets but not one of them is wearing a uniform?

She might have snatched up an ax like Mamie Long did and taken a swing at one of them, might then have ended up shot dead and sprawled across the woodpile like Mamie Long. She might have gone crazy like Bessie and lunged at a man, tried to knock him down, take his gun, bite a chunk out of his arm, fight for her life. Fight back, and you're already dead; you might as well go out fighting.

On the October Sunday after the Longs were killed, she fastened her large black hat in front of the mirror beside her front door, while Zeke paced the floor and told her what was happening all over town. White men were going door to door, telling the white people that the colored people had guns and knives hidden in their houses. Sheriff's deputies were stopping colored people on the street, asking where they'd been and where they were going. Zeke had been stopped himself a few times. It was best to stay inside.

"No ignorant cracker is going to keep me from going to church," she said. "You'd do well to come with me."

While she pinned her hat, he went on talking. He'd be damned if he was going to worship any God who'd turned his face away from them the way this God had done. "You don't know anything, Mama, if you think God's going to protect you," he said.

"I know you'd better stop blaspheming," she said, but there was no way to stop him once he got wound up. The way it looked to him, he said, the Almighty had turned his back on the colored people of South Carolina a long time ago. Hell, he might even have *given* the whole state to the devil. "Go on, Satan, take it," God said, and the devil answered, "Sure thing, Boss, much obliged."

It always grieved her when he talked like that. She took down her black patent leather purse from a nail on the wall and checked the folded dollars there. "You better hush about the devil," she said.

She didn't believe in the actual devil any longer; Dr. Scott, the pastor at Mt. Hebron Baptist Church, wasn't big on the devil either, though he sometimes preached on his many names and disguises. *Accuser of the Brethren. Ruler of Darkness. Tempter. Thief. Father of Lies.* At church on the terrible Sunday after the killings, some of the old people swore that during the night they'd felt the devil's heavy cloak dragged over the town, but Dr. Scott admonished them not to give in to fear and superstition. He led them in singing: "Father, I stretch my hand to thee, no other help I know."

"Have salt in yourselves," he said in his lordly voice, "and be at peace with one another."

Then they took up a special offering for Mr. N. R. Latham, an offering that Dr. Scott allowed but would not personally contribute to. Others blamed N. R. Latham as well and gave nothing, but she dropped a dollar in the basket for the man who'd torn such a big hole in the case against the three Longs that Dempsey stepped through it and went free. He was halfway to Monetta, so they'd heard, when the sheriff got him.

One last silence filled: Dempsey Long's hour of freedom on the day the judge dismissed the verdict against him.

He might have stood up from his seat at the front of the courtroom, but N. R. Latham grabbed his wrist and pulled him back down onto the hard bench beside him and held on to keep him there. He would have known why Dempsey shouldn't stand up, why he must stop smiling. But Dempsey couldn't stop. He didn't want to leave Bessie and Albert in jail, but he was free. It wouldn't do any good to wait around until tomorrow when they might be, and it could do harm.

"Thank you, sir," he said to N. R. Latham. He shook the man's hand, shook it again. Latham took him by the elbow, turned him away from the courtroom, where groups of white men had gathered in corners to talk and glance over their shoulders at the two of them. "If you don't have any more business in town, Dempsey," he said, "why don't you go home? Go cross-country if you can. Head on back to your people."

What people? he wanted to ask. *What home?* The lawyer knew that his family was dead or scattered like a fire when you kick the last embers to make sure it's out. He'd seen his mother sprawled across the woodpile, dead, his wife Clara running across a field with the baby in her arms. He would have known that no Long lived there any longer, but he might have hoped he was wrong and started for home. Where else would he go? Where do any of us go after we've lost everything? The sun was low in the sky, the light fading fast, but he would walk all night if he had to; the dark didn't scare him like it had scared his mother. She wouldn't go into a lightless house, so she'd always quit work in plenty of time to get home and light the lamps and rouse the fire. But he wasn't afraid. He should have been dead for over a year, and instead he was free, walking north toward Monetta and home, enjoying the way the setting sun left a band of cold peach light along the horizon. In the stands of scrub oak and pine beyond the fields it was already night, the last light fading over the open ground. It was the time of day when his father had always come into the shed where he was putting up the mule, hanging up the harness; he'd turn and squint at the sun then look back at Dempsey, measuring one against the other. If he spat on the ground after looking, Dempsey had quit too early. If his father nodded or patted the mule's dusty neck, it meant that the day's work was done to the old man's satisfaction and they could both go home and rest.

18

Ezekial Settles

1980

FROM HIS SEAT at the head of his mother's casket, he can see the whole of Mt. Hebron Baptist Church. The tall windows he washed this morning; the worn oak pews; the deep-red carpet that runs along the center aisle from the pulpit through the open doors at the back and down the steps into the bright sunlight beyond. People move into the church out of the brightness and must stop to let their eyes adjust to the dim interior; the change is that drastic. The old people, especially, have to stand there for a while to get their bearings, and it's mostly the old who have come to his mother's home-going, so there's considerable delay and confusion at the back of the church. Then more confusion as the elders totter up the aisle and are met with the sight of Zeke Settles keeping watch beside a closed casket, and they have to stop again and shake their heads, to adjust their thinking. Behind him the choir rustles, a flock of satin birds.

What they think doesn't matter. What matters is that he promised his mother he'd go with her as far as he could go, and sitting beside her casket with his hand up under the spray of red roses, her favorite flower, is one way he's keeping that promise. The closed casket is another; she hadn't wanted to be stared at. He chose the pecan wood casket, the most expensive in Jackson's salesroom, in honor of his mother's love of pecans, the way she could crack two Gloria Grandes in one hand and slip the whole meat from the shell. From where he sits, he can see his wife Denise and their two girls, married women now with children of their own, looking back at him from the front pew.

He watches Denise bring her thirty years of experience as a junior high school mathematics teacher to totaling the cost of casket and roses, and when she looks at him again, he sees she's already at work on how they will pay for it, and he smiles at her gratefully.

In the pew behind his family the Daughters of Zion fan themselves with square cardboard fans printed with a picture of Jesus in the Garden of Gethsemane, beseeching his father to take the cup of suffering from him. They are dressed all in white, with red sashes across their chests, like the one his mother will wear into eternity, as she wanted. Some white people have come too, and they sit together halfway back on the left-hand side of the church. He checks the roses on the casket to make sure that none have wilted, and he looks up again to see the Aimars step in out of the light: Lewis, Libba, and a younger woman, Lewis's daughter no doubt; she looks just like him. Of course they're here, he thinks. They'd better be.

Mrs. Aimar wears a black suit and a small pillbox hat, but her hair looks untidy, poking out from under, and her skirt is twisted so the zipper shows. She shuffles in on Lewis's arm, wearing on her feet what look to be velvet bedroom slippers. How are the mighty fallen. The younger woman wears a plain black dress, and her light hair falls straight to her shoulders. She has the shrewd blue Aimar eyes, the long thin nose and narrow family face. Seeing him, Mrs. Aimar brightens, shakes loose from Lewis and starts up the aisle, her purse gaping open and swinging from her arm. She walks as if she's falling forward. *Get up off that seat and go help her,* his mother says. *Aren't you ashamed of yourself?* He starts to obey, but Lewis catches up with his mother, snaps her purse shut, speaks to her. In her raised chin, the vehement movement of her mouth, he sees the ghost of the woman she'd been, and his heart jumps and starts to pound, the way it used to do when she called him: "Zeke, you Zeke, come here this minute."

The wife of the man who pointed a gun at him and ran him out of town. That's how he's thought of her since the day it happened, and even though his mother swore that Howard Aimar saved his life by running him off, Zeke will stick with what he remembers: Aimar's eyes, the gun aimed at his heart, and Curtis N. R. Barrett protesting quietly, then not at all, until the only difference between the two of them came down to which one held the gun. Later, when Howard Aimar had gone inside, Barrett had handed him a New York address scribbled on a scrap of paper, and Zeke made sure he'd seen him drop it on the ground before he left the Aimars' yard for the last time.

As his heart slows, he realizes he'd been afraid that Libba Aimar was going to try and give him the wren's nest again. One day long ago Libba had found the nest in the yard, strands of his mother's hair woven into it. She'd given it to Minnie as a testament, she'd said, to Minnie's place in their family. But when his mother quit and moved out a month after he went north, she left it on the shelf above her fireplace. Left it along with every cast-off blouse and winter coat, every chair and knickknack and dish towel, taking with her nothing but what she'd brought when she came to work for them. For years Mrs. Aimar had tried to give the nest back to Minnie. She'd nestled it among the oranges, divinity, roasted pecans, and fruitcake in the yearly Christmas basket. Once she'd even tucked it into a basket of ironing, but his mother had sent it back on top of the tissue paper she always laid over her finished work.

This remembering is exactly why it is not good for him to come here. The sleeping wrongs kicked awake; the shut-up rooms opened; the return of a disheartening sense of what his life has cost him. What his mother's life cost her. He doesn't have to be here long before the husband, father, grandfather, retired Pullman porter on the New York–Chicago line that he is in New York begins to collapse. The man who takes pleasure in the still-growing totals recorded in Denise's precise hand in the bankbook in the top drawer of the desk in their bedroom, who believes that their steady increase tracks not just a growing prosperity but a widening distance between the man he'd become in New York and the one he used to be here. All it takes for that man to start to doubt himself is to step down from the train in Aiken and see the low spreading limbs of the live oak where he used to park his horse and wagon and wait for customers. By the time that man has walked a half a mile from the station to Toole Hill and set his suitcase on his mother's front porch and called and knocked and waited for her to unbolt, unchain, unlock, the door, he feels like he's come all this way to return a nice borrowed suit, put on his own clothes again, and turn back into himself: Zeke Settles, hat in hand, at your service.

The Aimars file into the front pew of the white section, and watching them, he realizes that the memory of the day he left Aiken is not finished with him yet. It was the morning after the flower show, and Howard Aimar had just bailed him out of jail and driven him to his mother's house, still wearing the white jacket he'd worn to serve supper the night before. A silent drive, he remembers. Something was wrong. He remembers the light sifting through the trees, a thread of smoke twisting up from his mother's chimney. He'd gone inside to show her that he was all right, and when he came back out, Curtis N. R. Barrett was hurrying down the driveway, topcoat flying. He and Howard Aimar exchanged a few sharp words, then Mr. Aimar walked right up close to Zeke and started in on him about the gray fedora he liked to wear tipped down over one eye, to give a little snap, a little flair, to the way he eyed a girl. Mr. Aimar seemed to bear that hat a special grudge; he was forever at him to take it off, straighten it up, get rid of it. His mother had warned him about waving the hat in a white man's face like a red flag in front of a bull, but as usual, he hadn't listened. "Zeke," he said. "I want you to set that hat straight on your head, and don't let me catch you wearing it like that again."

Zeke guessed that he was just showing off for Barrett, letting him know who was boss. So he said, "Yes, sir, Mr. Aimar," and he nudged the brim up a fraction of an inch and stood there, rocking back on his heels, grinning like a fool.

What happened next happened so fast that he can't slow it down, even now. To this day he's never seen a man move as fast as Howard Aimar did that morning: one continuous motion that carried him over to the green Ford and back, a pistol held down at his side. "Zeke," he said. "I'm going to ask you a question, and you'd better think very carefully before you answer me. Did you sell Mr. Barrett some of my whiskey?"

Nothing to say to that but the truth; it was clear he already knew.

"Yes, sir," he said.

"And did you show something of mine to Mr. Barrett?"

He remembers how the smoke stopped rising from his mother's chimney then; the chickens stopped pecking the ground; his mother, who'd just that minute stepped out onto her porch to bring him a clean shirt, dropped it and put a hand over her mouth; Curtis N. R. Barrett stood there in his black topcoat. Even the leaves on the big magnolia next to his mother's house stopped clattering and hung still.

He remembers the perfect silence, the stillness, and how he'd felt the answer rushing up his throat. *Your shoes with the blood on them?* He was free to say that and to be, for the first and last time in his life, an entirely free man. Over Howard Aimar's shoulder he saw his mother. She had taken her hand down from her mouth, and he will remember the look on her face forever. It was as if years of grieving had carved her face into a mask of mourning. "Yes, sir," he said, and his mother cried out, "He's a damn liar," and Howard Aimar raised the gun, thumbed back the hammer. For maybe half a minute they stood like that, and he watched Aimar's mind race through the choices.

Then he lowered the gun, eased the hammer down. "You don't work for me anymore, Zeke," he said. "I want you gone by the end of the day, and you don't set foot in this yard again." He was on the New York train that night.

Now he checks his watch: They're ten minutes behind schedule already because of the time it takes for all the old people to shuffle in and find seats. It is a muggy July afternoon, and two ancient black fans up front push thick air over the congregation. Around his mother's casket the floral tributes stand three deep: lilies and gardenias and more red roses from the Daughters of Zion. The largest offering, a cross covered in white carnations, is from Mrs. Howard Aimar and family, "With deepest sympathy." As the church heats up, the pews and the wooden ceiling beams creak and crack, the air fills with the smell of hot wood, starched clothes, pomade and perfume, gardenias and roses. Finally one of the ushers shuts the doors, and the preacher climbs into the pulpit, smiles down tenderly on his flock. He is a young man with a very round head and round glasses perched on a gentle face, new to the church this year. Minnie had liked him well enough, though she didn't go to church often enough anymore to get worked up one way or the other about the preacher. For the last ten years she'd gone to meetings of the Daughters of Zion, but on Sunday mornings she'd mostly stayed home. She liked to go out and sit under the crepe myrtle tree in her yard if it was warm or inside by the fire when it got cold. "And do what?" he'd asked.

"Think my own thoughts."

He'd never have predicted that old age would have carried her away so steadily or so far. He doesn't know what kind of old age he imagined and wished for her, only that it was easier than the one she'd lived. She wouldn't move to New York—they'd settled that question early—and *his* life was there—they'd settled that too—but for years, she'd come to New York at Christmas and again in the summer. On those visits she mostly sat by the front window, looking down onto the asphalt playground in the middle of the apartment block where they lived. She cooked and washed and ironed their clothes as fast and skillfully as she'd always done that work. She taught his girls to cook and iron too.

Then, ten years ago, she stopped coming. New York was too cold, she said. Too loud. Their tenth-floor apartment in Harlem was too far from the ground. She had bad dreams when she was there. Besides, she liked her little house in Aiken: the sandy yard she raked and swept, the two old tractor tires that she spruced up with a fresh coat of white paint every spring then planted with zinnias. She couldn't skip a day setting out a potful of grits, bacon grease, and crumbled biscuits for the stray dogs that counted on her. As she got older and more hardheaded, those dogs became the main reason she wouldn't come to see them, and the fact that she'd chosen a pack of mongrels over him and his family had hurt him more than any of the other excuses. But he didn't let it show. He installed a telephone in her house, and they talked every Sunday. Every summer he went south on the train to visit her for two weeks, taking one of his girls with him.

It wasn't that her mind stumbled either. Until her heart began to fail, she remembered his phone number. She knew the names, ages, and birthdays of his daughters and their children, and on each of their birthdays a card always arrived with a dollar tucked inside, "From your ever-loving Grandmother," written in a hand that only last year began to wobble. Nonetheless, she'd left them, like someone rowing steadily away, not looking back at the shore. He thought he knew her better than that, but toward the end he wondered if she'd always been this solitary, unreachable person.

He remembers lying in his narrow bed in her house in the Aimar's backyard, listening to the creak of the ironing board as she leaned into her work, the clunk of one iron being set back on the woodstove to heat before she picked up another, the small hiss as she wet her finger and touched it. The smell of cloth, metal, starch. When she ironed on muggy summer nights, he slept on the back porch, away from the unbearable heat inside.

"Mama," he says once, under his breath, feeling the smooth wood of her casket, knowing he'd better not say it again, because to name who she was is to name what is gone, and once that absence began to spread, it could go on forever.

The church is quiet now, the old people all seated and settled. He looks out over the nodding hats on the unsteady old heads, the square cardboard fans from Jackson's waggling through the air. "Though the fig tree does not blossom," the preacher begins, "nor fruit be on the vines, the labor of the olive fail and the fields yield no food, the flock be cut off from the fold and there be no herd in the stalls, yet I will rejoice in the Lord.

"Habakkuk, the author of this verse, is called one of the minor prophets, but he bears a major message. I am weighed down with misery and failure, he says. Turned out into the dark to stagger blindly through the world, so heavy laden I cannot lift up my head to see the road ahead. And yet, the prophet says, and *yet,* I will rejoice in the Lord. Do you hear the joyful noise, the mighty sound of that simple word, my brothers and sisters? Do you hear glory's trumpets in the prophet's fateful word? And *yet.* Do you hear the stone rumble as it's rolled away from the tomb? And yet, he says, I will not simply endure, I will *rejoice.* Our sister Minnie lived her life in the shelter of those mighty words."

"Yes she did," a Daughter of Zion calls out.

"She bore that weight of which the prophet speaks, and now she has gone home to a place where the harvest is bountiful and every tree is laden with fruit and the labor of the olive is done."

"Amen."

"Last night her son Ezekial shared with me some of the facts of our sister's life. Perhaps you already know them. She was born in the country up near Edgefield, and after her father died, her mother brought the family to town so her children could attend the Schofield School.

"Let us give thanks now for the mothers. For those who labor through the long nights, through the long days and years so that their children may go on to places they have never traveled."

"Amen," Zeke says. He pats the casket lid and feels his mother's absence widen inside him again. Mrs. Aimar nods and smiles around her, like she's the one being praised, and Lewis puts his arm around her shoulder. Another sleeping wrong stirs and rouses: the way white people act like the sun shines on them alone and every word of praise rings to their glory.

"Last night Ezekial told me many things about our sister. He told me how she graduated from the Schofield School and that her domestic skills were beyond compare, how these skills carried them both until he was able to make his own way. He told me that she raised him to be the man he is today and of her lifelong membership, her leadership, in the Daughters of Zion, and as a pillar of this church."

Not exactly true, he thinks, but comforting to those who believed it. Like the meek little smile the undertaker set on his mother's mouth. No doubt that was meant to comfort the living too. He'd asked, then insisted, that the undertaker fix it; he didn't want to think of her smiling through eternity like she was saying, "Yes, ma'am." He'll apologize to the mortician later; the man was just doing his job, trying to ease the sorrow of the living by making the dead look as if they'd had no quarrel with life.

"And Ezekial told me something else about our sister as well. Something many of you younger people, myself included, may not know, though the elders will no doubt recall it. I'm speaking of the night in the fall of 1926 when three of our people were dragged from the county jail and murdered."

The hats on the old heads are moving now, shaking slowly, to and fro. *Lord. Lord. Lord.*

"The next day, while many huddled in their houses, Mrs. Settles and another member of the Daughters of Zion went to Mr. Jackson's parlor, bringing clothes for the murdered three. And being there so struck by the horror of what lay before their eyes, the other woman fled, and our sister found herself so weak she could only sit in a chair in the corner while Mr. Jackson went about his labors with the clothes she'd brought." The church is very quiet now; even the cardboard fans have stopped. The old people sit with bowed heads. His wife and daughters, to whom he has never told this story, watch him, worried. Latitia, his oldest daughter, looks at the ceiling, holding back tears.

Mrs. Aimar whispers to Lewis, who pats her on the shoulder, puts a finger to his lips. He looks puzzled, troubled, and it occurs to Zeke that his mother might have been right to say that Lewis Aimar had never heard any story but his mother's about that time or his father's complicity. And Libba Aimar herself might never have known why Zeke was there one day and gone the next. On that fateful morning she'd been at her cousin's place in the country. Who knows what Howard Aimar told her about Zeke's disappearance when she returned. Whatever it was, she would have believed him.

Lewis's daughter watches him intently. He remembers what his mother said about that one. She and her first husband had gotten down on their luck and come home, and Lewis Aimar had put them to work on the rich man's estate that he'd started managing after the war, when he took over his father's business and shouldered his debts. "After Mister died, the Aimars were poor as church mice," Minnie always said, not without pleasure. Lewis put his daughter with the cleaning crew, and the husband worked on the grounds. His mother was the boss of the crew that put the houses in top shape before the wealthy northerners came to town in the spring. Lewis's girl came and went as she pleased, Minnie said, took as long as she wanted to for lunch, but what could she do? Fire Mr. Lewis's daughter? When she worked, she worked hard. She'd get down on her hands and knees and scrub the baseboards along with everybody else. She didn't remember how it came up, but they talked about the Long killings once, and his daughter asked all sorts of questions. Said she suspected that her grandfather had a hand in the thing. Someday, he thinks, they might be able to talk to one another, but not yet.

"Ezekial says that she told him once about that terrible night," the preacher says, "about the undertaker's room and the common grave where the three of them were buried, and then she never spoke of it again. That was some of the weight our sister carried through life." The preacher bows his head, and he keeps it bowed for a minute or more. Then he begins to nod, slowly at first, then more emphatically, as though he's won some argument with himself. "And yet," he says, his voice rising. "And YET. Thank God our sister lived to see the world turn a little bit away from that darkness and toward the light of the prophet's ringing words."

"Amen," another Daughter shouts.

"And yet, our sister rejoiced in the Lord. The journey is ever the same, my brothers and sisters, for those who love the Lord. Though we walk through the valley of the shadow, we come at last to the Lord. Though the tomb be sealed, the stone is rolled away. Though the labor of the olive fail and the fig tree does not blossom, we rejoice in the Lord. We rejoice."

"Is that what you were doing?" he imagines himself whispering to her, the way he'd often done in this very church when he was a child. "Were you rejoicing in the Lord when you stopped coming to see us? Is that what you were doing out under the crepe myrtle on those Sunday mornings with your pack of stray dogs at your feet?"

While the choir sways and sings "Precious Lord," he helps carry his mother's casket to the back of the church and set it on a stand, so that people can file past on their way out and say their last good-byes. So many old ladies kiss and hug him that his face and collar are soon smeared with lipstick. When her time comes, Mrs. Aimar holds onto one of the coffin handles like she's taking it with her. Lewis and his daughter have to pry her fingers loose and lead her away.

Outside the air is smothering, the light bright as tin. Thunderheads race toward them from the west. They will have to hurry to the cemetery on Toole Hill to outrun the storm. Or maybe the lightning and the rain will beat them there, and they'll get to keep her on earth a little longer. He puts on his dark glasses, stands behind the hearse while Jackson's men slide his mother's casket in. He helps his wife and daughters into the car from Jackson's. Maybe he can get in, too, before the Aimars catch up with him. Maybe he can ride away without having to speak to them.

"Zeke?" No one here calls him that, except for them. He stops, turns. Today he's doing what his mother would have wanted; she would have been polite, so he will be polite. Maybe that was where she went, he thinks. All those years of being mannerly gave her a lot of practice in keeping her distance, and finally she just walked off into it.

Lewis Aimar extends his hand, and he takes it. "Sorry about your mother, Zeke," he says. "Sorry for your loss. I remember her fondly; we all do. She was a fine person, and we'll miss her."

Lewis Aimar has squint lines around his eyes, the open face of a man with few regrets and nothing to hide. He looks Zeke in the eye, as though there's only goodwill between them. Goodwill and good memories of himself as a little boy, riding all over town in Zeke's wagon.

"Thank you," he says.

"You know my daughter Elizabeth?"

"I do not," he says. "How do you do?"

She shakes his hand as well. "I'm sorry about your mother," she says. Her look is keener, the presumption of goodwill not so apparent.

"Thank you." For once, he thinks, Libba Aimar is waiting her turn. Up close she looks more bedraggled and blank than she did in church. Picked threads on her suit jacket, a loose button dangling. His mother kept herself up. Sorting through her clothes, he hadn't found one unmended rip, one missing button or sagging hem. It makes him proud to remember that, proud and fierce and superior: *You've gotten pitiful, and my mother never did.* But right behind that feeling comes another one. He remembers hearing from one of the Daughters of Zion that before he came down to look after his mother, Libba Aimar had visited every day, bringing homemade soup and flowers from her garden. She'd sit with her for hours, they said. And that is the essence of the problem with being here: how confusing everything became when you weren't studying this place from a distance; you were down in it, part of it again, if only for a little while.

"Ezekial," she says. She holds out both hands, her head held to one side in the old, charming way, and there's nothing to do but take her hands in his own. "I'm sorry it took this sad occasion to bring you home."

She looks haggard and hollow, with the same look in her eyes he saw in his mother's in her final days: a dark presence regarding him from far away. It won't be long, he thinks, before her people will gather in a different church to see her off, but—the thought pours over him like cool water—he won't be among them. He will not come back here again. He tries to pull his hands free, but she holds on.

"We will miss your dear mother," she says. "She was so good to me. She was so . . ." He waits while she bites her bottom lip and rummages for the word, fear in her eyes, as though she's forgotten where she is or what she's doing there. The loose skin of her hands slides over the thin bones, and he squeezes her hands to show he's listening.

". . . so good and true," she says.

As soon as she says it, something inside him slams shut to keep it out, but it slips through anyway, and he's aware that she hasn't come close to saying what he wants to hear. He doesn't know exactly what it will be, only that he will know it when he hears it, and he hasn't heard it yet. He only knows that she is stronger than any confused old woman with one foot in the grave has a right to be, and she still won't let go of his hands.

Acknowledgments

Many people helped, guided, and supported me throughout the process of researching and writing this book. I would like to thank the following individuals and institutions:

The Virginia Center for the Creative Arts, for several residencies during which this book was written and revised.

The Department of English and Comparative Literature at the University of North Carolina and its chair, Beverly Taylor, for granting me a research leave at a crucial point in the writing.

The Institute of the Arts and Humanities at the University of North Carolina, where I spent a semester in good conversation with colleagues during the formative stages of imagining this book.

Aaron Marcus, for his skillful research into Oliver H. P. Garrett's reporting for the New York World.

Alan Shapiro, John Rosenthal, and Ann Loftin, friends to the manuscript and to me.

The late George Garrett, for generously sharing written material and recollections of his uncle, Oliver H. P. Garrett.

Fitzhugh Brundage, for an early conversation that helped to orient me to my subject.

Jan Nordby Gretlund, for honoring my work in Denmark and for all his help over the years in keeping my work visible.

Michael Griffith, extraordinary editor, whose questions and challenges helped to make the prose cleaner, the insights sharper.

Peter Perlman, whose love, care, support, and encouragement mean everything to me.

I am so grateful to you all.